Kamigawa Cycle · Book II

HERETIC

Betrayers
of kamigawa

Scott McGough

WIZARDS
OF THE COAST

F/ M^cG
T06113

HERETIC: BETRAYERS OF KAMIGAWA

©2005 Wizards of the Coast, Inc.

Cover art by Chris Moeller
First Printing: January 2005
Library of Congress Catalog Card Number: 2004113601

9 8 7 6 5 4 3 2 1

US ISBN: 0-7869-3575-8
ISBN-13: 978-0-7869-3575-8
620-17630-001-EN

U.S., CANADA,
ASIA, PACIFIC, & LATIN AMERICA
Wizards of the Coast, Inc.
P.O. Box 707
Renton, WA 98057-0707
+1-800-324-6496

EUROPEAN HEADQUARTERS
Wizards of the Coast, Belgium
T Hofveld 6d
1702 Groot-Bijgaarden
Belgium
+322 467 3360

Visit our web site at www.wizards.com

To save a kingdom, he must betray its king.

Toshi Umezawa has never been a particularly religious man.
Nor has he particularly cared about the affairs of others. The
path of the errant ronin has ever been a solitary one, and he is as
surprised as any when the dangerous attentions of the myojin, a
princess, and the moon folk all involved in a secret the daimyo
would kill to protect would change all that. And amid all the
confusion, the attacks of the kami against the daimyo's kingdom, and against Toshi himself, are getting worse.

**Scott McGough continues an epic story of a ronin and a
princess and the strange turns their unlikely alliance takes
as they attempt to discover the truth behind the kami's war.**

EXPERIENCE THE MAGIC™

PART ONE

PRAYERS
FOR A WINTER NIGHT

Softly falls the snow
Blanketing fears, stilling hearts
Sleep, carry me home

All Towabara was abuzz. For the first time in years, Daimyo Konda would address his subjects directly from the steps of his mighty tower. The official proclamations were vague as to the content of this address, but they were very clear about its importance. Any able-bodied adult who did not attend would be called before the daimyo's feared civil enforcers, his *go-yo* squads, to explain why.

On the eve of the address, four armed soldiers retrieved Lady Pearl-Ear of the *kitsunebito* from her cell in the tower's upper chambers. They surrounded the small fox-woman as they marched down to ground level, but they always kept a respectful distance. If not for the clank of heavy iron chains around her wrists and ankles, the silent retainers would have seemed more an honor guard than jailers.

Pearl-Ear herself remained stoic and inscrutable, her wide eyes calm and her short-muzzled face held high. The chains did not noticeably hamper her graceful movements, though she was thin-boned and delicate under her white robes and pale gray fur. She furrowed her brow in annoyance when the metal links audibly scraped against one another, but otherwise she gave no sign that she was even aware of her bonds.

The gate sentries saw the strange procession coming and opened the outer door. The sky above the courtyard was a dull, dusty yellow, and a stifling haze had descended. In the shadow of the great tower, the air was cool but stale, and it pressed on Pearl-Ear like a wet canvas.

Her escorts led the way to a larger collection of Konda's retainers in their finest dress uniforms. Pearl-Ear, who had been a member of the daimyo's court for more than twenty years, recognized none of the soldiers she saw. No surprise there: Konda was unlikely to assign watchdog duty to any soldier who knew and might sympathize with her. Although this was merely more evidence of her sad fall from the daimyo's good graces, Pearl-Ear reserved her pity for the soldiers themselves.

The Kami War had taken a heavy toll on all of Kamigawa, but it was the daimyo's retainers who had paid most dearly and most often. Of the thousands of soldiers assembled, Pearl-Ear calculated that more than a third had no military experience whatsoever and had been recruited simply to maintain the ranks.

Eiganjo Fortress included the tower and the walled courtyard around it. It functioned as a small city where civilian merchants and artisans conducted business alongside billeted soldiers and officers of the daimyo's army. Farmers, tourists, and foreign dignitaries came and went on a daily basis. In better times, there was a constant flow of goods and people to and from the tower.

After twenty years of war, Eiganjo was not so much a fortress as a last safe haven. Daimyo Konda's citizens and retainers lived crammed behind the tower walls like refugees. The only movement now was one way, into the city, then into the ranks of the daimyo's army. There was a massive stable at the far end of the compound, currently half-empty. The vast expanse of arable plains to the north was barren, its fields either fallow or victims of assaults from the spirit realm.

Pearl-Ear straightened her back, struggling to keep her face from reflecting the misery she felt around her. The mighty walls of Eiganjo had become as much of a prison to the daimyo's people as they were to her.

As her eyes adjusted to the gloom and the haze, Pearl-Ear continued to hold her head high. Two decades of marauding spirits had reduced a once-thriving population to the haggard throng now assembled outside the tower gates. Where Konda had once been master of a realm that covered most of the continent and bordered on every other powerful lord's domain, now his entire kingdom was easily contained inside a single fortress. A nation of almost a quarter million had been reduced to well under a hundred thousand. The rest had either fallen to marauding kami or had fled when it became clear that Konda's kingdom was the front line of the war between the *kakuriyo* spirit world and the *utsushiyo* human one. Most of those who remained were now waiting outside the tower. Even Pearl-Ear, the disgraced former tutor of the daimyo's daughter, was mustered out for Konda's address.

Pearl-Ear craned her head back and tried to see to the tower's highest window, looking for any sign of Princess Michiko. The sulfurous haze prevented her, and she blinked away tears as she lowered her gaze. If she herself was obliged to attend the daimyo's address, wouldn't Michiko? Wouldn't the daimyo release his own daughter from her cell as he had the fox-woman?

Pearl-Ear could not credit the daimyo with the callousness it would take to exclude his only child, but then again, she could not credit his imprisoning Michiko in the first place. A few short months ago, Princess Michiko had secretly left the tower in direct disobedience of her father and her tutor, exposing herself to the myriad and very real dangers of the Kami War and the open countryside. Disastrous circumstances prevented Pearl-Ear from bringing Michiko-hime back immediately, and when they did return Konda's forbearance had melted like a cobweb in a blacksmith's forge. He blamed Pearl-Ear for the string of catastrophes that had occurred while Michiko was outside his protection, and he was furious at Michiko for defying him.

Even now, Pearl-Ear could understand Konda's anger but not his inability to control it. He locked his daughter in one of the tallest rooms in the tower and threw Pearl-Ear into a cell of her own far below. Pearl-Ear, who had stayed on as a kitsune ambassador to Konda's court for decades precisely to be with Michiko-hime, was now barred from seeing the princess . . . or anyone else, save the soldiers who guarded her.

The sudden beating of a heavy drum interrupted Pearl-Ear's thoughts, and a murmur went through the crowd. The soldiers all snapped to attention without the slightest sound or glance from their officers. The air seemed to vibrate throughout the courtyard. Daimyo Konda was coming.

The great double doors swung wide, and a procession of heralds marched through in lines of three. The first row wore huge drums bound across their chests. The second three carried short poles, between which hung a long bolt of cloth with Konda's sun and moon standard woven in. The final trio, young girls in white robes, scattered white flowers behind them as they exited the tower.

There was a pause as the last few petals fluttered to the dusty ground. Then, Daimyo Konda himself emerged to the thunderous roars of his army, accompanied by his most trusted general and a small platoon of bodyguards.

Konda was well into his seventies, but he hadn't visibly aged since the birth of his daughter twenty years past. His long white hair almost glowed in the dim light, cascading past his shoulders. His beard and mustache were likewise white, healthy, and strong, following every turn of his head like a long cavalry banner at full gallop. He was dressed in a fine robe of gold brocade with dazzling silver moons embroidered across its front.

In the poor light and the great distance Konda's eyes seemed perfectly normal, but Pearl-Ear knew his pupils floated and meandered around the sockets like blind fish in a bowl. Even when he had condemned her to her lonely cell, even when his face was mere inches away and all his attention was focused on her, his eyes drifted lazily back and forth, sometimes floating outside the boundaries of his face. Much had changed about Konda during the twenty years of war with the kakuriyo.

Pearl-Ear tore her gaze from Konda long enough to verify what her ears told her was true: though the citizens of Towabara shouted and stamped their feet along with the soldiers, their fervor was hollow and listless. Their situation was too grave and Konda had been too long detached from the lives of his people. He had once been the nation's greatest joy, but all Pearl-Ear sensed now from the people was the painful weight of desperation and a dour wave of fear. Whatever their ruler had gathered them to say, she prayed that it would give the people hope.

His herald called for silence. Konda stepped up to a podium and raised his arms wide.

"Children of Towabara," he said, his voice deep and powerful. "You are all welcome here. As cruel fate has deprived me of my own daughter's trust, I take great solace in the love and obedience you have shown me today.

"I have brought you here to reassure you—not by words, but by demonstration. Our enemies are strong. They are numerous, and relentless. It is the power of our nation that excites them, the fear that we will become more powerful than they. When I began to unify the tribes and city-states of this land under my protection, other great daimyo behaved in exactly the same manner. They would rather attack than accept the wisdom of joining a greater cause, would rather viciously and spitefully wound the great state that seeks to lift them up. The kami and great myojin of the spirit world are frightened, my people. Frightened of you and me and the strength we represent. I thought I could turn aside their fear and their anger long enough for them to see our inevitable victory, for we are the future of Kamigawa. I thought this, but I was wrong."

Audible gasps of disbelief ran through the crowd. Konda gripped the podium and leaned forward.

"Yes, my children, wrong. The armies of the kakuriyo have abandoned any semblance of honorable warfare. They strike from ambush without warning, without regard to youth or innocence. Recent events have proven that they will stop at nothing, not even the use of their ultimate weapon on troops performing a mission of mercy in the name of a father's love . . ."

Konda's loud voice trailed off, and his mind seemed to wander as his eyes drifted across his face.

"What about the Spirit Beast?" someone shouted. "Three thousand dead in a single stroke and a hundred acres swallowed whole. We all felt the tremor, Great Lord. What power do we have in the face of that?"

The speaker had dared too much. Pearl-Ear had pinpointed the man's position in the crowd seconds before the soldiers nearby fell on him and rendered him silent.

"My brother died in that folly, daimyo."

"And mine. No one can tell me how or why."

"Do you even know, Konda?"

The voices began to come from all around the courtyard, faster than the guards could find and muffle them. The daimyo had claimed the kami were frightened, but Pearl-Ear heard true fear in the voices of Konda's subjects as they cried out for their sons, brothers, wives, and sisters who had fallen.

A flash of bright white light crackled across Konda's body. "Enough." Though his voice was smooth and even, it was loud enough to shake the fortress walls and drive half the audience to their knees.

Among the groans and gasps, Konda continued. "I will not be shouted at by you rabble like an absent-minded servant. We have all suffered from this war. Why this has happened is not as important as our response.

"I am your lord and master, and more, I am your protector. I have assessed the threats we face, new and old, and I have devised our answer to those threats." He raised and lowered his arm, and the drummers beat out a new tattoo. Across the courtyard, the great main gates opened to reveal a massive company of mounted soldiers. Beyond the cavalry, five thousand infantry stood at the ready.

"The go-yo and the Eiganjo battalion have proven themselves capable of protecting this city. The rest of my army will ride forth into Kamigawa, driving the kami before them. No longer will my retainers sit and wait to be attacked. If the kakuriyo seeks total warfare, we will fight it on our terms, not theirs."

With a grand flourish, Konda waved his arms. A line of strange shapes soared out from behind the tower, matching rows of twelve on each side. With their huge, flat wings gracefully beating the air, huge moths spread out over the courtyard below, the pale yellow light glittering on their powdered wings. From their specially designed saddles, armored moth riders guided their steeds through their circling pattern as they soared and looped overhead.

The daimyo paused, and Pearl-Ear realized he was waiting for a reaction from the crowd. He was expecting a surge of applause, a riotous cheer from ten thousand grateful throats. Instead, not even the soldiers responded. Most were too busy eyeing the crowd, eager to pounce on anyone who broke the silence with more catcalls. The rest looked as pale and as frightened as their civilian peers.

Konda's face darkened. He raised one fist and the white light crackled around him once more. "Behold," he cried. "The kami send their most titanic beast to crush our resolve. When that beast comes again, it will not face mounted cavalry. Mere men cannot stand against the ultimate expression of the spirit world's ire. No, to protect us against the marauding kami and the hostile myojin, I give my children Yosei, the Morning Star, mighty spirit dragon, guardian of the Eiganjo and all its loyal citizens."

Konda's fist opened. The stale air above the courtyard began to spin. It formed a dense ball of yellow fog, illuminated from within by the same crackling light that adorned the daimyo. The fog thickened and spread, rising higher into the yellow sky until it was as large as the courtyard. As it passed over the moths, the great insects shuddered.

The spirit dragon Yosei burst from the fog like a snake slithering free of its leathery egg. He was long and slender. His forearms were folded flat along his streamlined body, and his scales bristled along his spine. His head was round, but his snout was flat and broad with whisker-like barbels on each side of his wide lips.

The white dragon coiled himself like a spring, spiraling higher until his hind legs and tail pulled free of the foggy dome. When he was whole and clear, Yosei's head darted down into the column created by his own coils. He emerged barely fifty yards over Konda, and there the great dragon stopped.

The daimyo gazed up, as did every other person in the courtyard. Pearl-Ear glanced at Konda then back up at Yosei, captivated by the huge beast. The dragon's barbels resembled Konda's long mustache, and when the daimyo nodded, the dragon nodded back.

Yosei's head shot forward toward the open gate. The rest of his long, graceful form followed the exact path of his head, curving down and around itself until the tip of his tail vanished through the gate and rose into the sky, out of sight. A trail of dust and yellow fog followed in his wake for a second, then dispersed.

"Yosei will not rest," Konda declared, "until he finds and destroys the Great Spirit Beast. In sending their most dreadful spirit against us, the kami have shown us their true power. I cannot allow such a display to go unanswered, and I will not allow another loyal subject of this realm to die when I can meet their greatest force with an even greater one.

"For Yosei serves me, as I serve you, and together we shall

defeat our enemy. The kakuriyo is in its death-throes. When it is done thrashing, our entire nation will stand supreme."

Now the soldiers did cheer, and soon the citizens joined in, swept along by the fervor Yosei inspired. A chant of "Konda, Konda!" rose over the cheers, and the daimyo bowed his head. The drummers began to play an exit processional. Konda turned and disappeared into the tower, followed by his bodyguards. In the courtyard, the crowd and soldiers continued to exult.

Pearl-Ear did not share their joy. Instead, she peered upward once more, straining in vain for a glimpse of Michiko-hime in the tower above.

* * * * *

Princess Michiko was not at the window of her lavishly furnished cell during her father's address. She did not see the crowds, the soldiers, or the dragon, and though her thoughts often turned to Lady Pearl-Ear, she did not look for her tutor through the thick haze outside.

Instead, Michiko sat at her writing desk, busily inscribing the same complicated symbol on a blank scroll with a stiff-bristled brush. Lost in concentration, she muttered to herself as she traced the same lines over and over until the ink-soaked paper all but dissolved under her efforts.

She had seen no one but soldiers since her imprisonment—not her father, not her tutor, not her most intimate friend. She was well fed and given free access to any books in her father's library, provided he approved them beforehand. She had read voraciously over the long months of her captivity, first a series of historical tomes about Kamigawa then scholarly texts about different spiritual practices. The daimyo had refused to supply any information she requested on the kami war, but he seemed content to let her complete her formal education on her own.

Apart from her books, Michiko was completely cut off from the outside world. The castle was well warded against any spells that might be cast to communicate with her, and the physical barriers of wall and sentry deterred any other kind of contact. Her friends, her mentor, her servants, and her father were all out of reach.

Michiko continued to trace the symbol. Fortunately, she had made acquaintances that her father didn't know about. One of her books detailed the practices of kanji magicians, who used special symbols to focus their magic. A seasoned kanji mage could burn wood by carving the symbol for fire into it or induce fever by chalking the right character on her victim's front door. By combining different symbols into the same kanji, even more powerful spells were possible.

The princess glanced down at the disintegrating sheet of parchment, still muttering to herself. When she had started practicing, she would often stop after the symbol for "messenger" before going on to the kanji for *hyozan*, or "iceberg." Since taking her brush in hand several hours ago, she had not paused at all, blending the two symbols together in a series of smooth, practiced motions, chanting all the while.

The symbol under her brush twitched. Michiko's eyes widened, but she kept tracing and chanting. It was beginning to work. She struggled to remain calm and to keep her rhythm steady.

There was a wet cracking sound as the kanji tore itself free of the paper and rose into the air. Michiko slid back in her chair, unwilling to breathe for fear of disrupting the ritual. She edged over so that she was between the floating symbol and the open window.

The messenger symbol did not try to leave, however, but floated before her as if waiting. Michiko took a breath and spoke softly, but clearly.

"Find him in the Takenuma Swamp," she said. "I have a new commission for him and his reckoners."

The symbol bobbed in the air. Michiko drew another breath and went on.

"Tell him I am in my father's tower. I am a prisoner. Rescue me, and the reward will stagger the greediest of hearts." Michiko paused, remembering her previous encounter with this would-be savior. "Even his.

"Go now," she said. "Tell Toshi that I will be waiting for him."

The messenger symbol rotated in the air before the princess then shot out of the open window and disappeared into the gloom.

CHAPTER 2

Toshi Umezawa sat at the bar in one of the worst taverns the world had ever known. Most of the buildings in Takenuma Swamp were grim, but The Rat's Nest was in a class by itself. The cups were filthy, the wine was foul, and the clientele was criminally insane. It was perched up on bamboo stilts like every other establishment in the Numai section of the swamp, but the Nest's east end had sunk far deeper into the muck so that foul, oily water lapped at the patron's feet at one end of the room.

There were only two things on the menu: a grayish rice wine that tended to strip the enamel off ceramic cups and a wad of unidentifiable meat on a stick. Apart from the *nezumi-bito* ratfolk, who could eat just about anything without retching, Toshi had never seen anyone take so much as a bite of the meat skewer without turning green and fouling himself.

Toshi mimed taking a sip of wine but poured the gray liquid on the floor instead. He surreptitiously filled the cup from the flask of water he wore on his belt then poured that out, too. Only then did he fill the cup again and drink. The wine residue was still too strong, though, and he grimaced as the noisome liquid burned his throat.

Toshi had spent a large part of his life convinced that he deserved better than he got, but this outing marked a milestone in his disappointment. I'm a newly spiritual man, he thought. Surely I shouldn't have to pray for a decent drink.

Around him, a handful of nezumi and human reprobates also made do with the extremely limited menu. None of the other patrons paid much attention to the average-looking fellow with the long hair and the samurai swords, which was one of the reasons he had chosen this bar and this district. Almost all of the fen residents were outlaws, thieves, or *ochimusha* like him. Unless he had stolen from them or they were planning to steal from him, they had no business to discuss.

The door opened to his left, and Toshi glanced at the newcomer. He smiled briefly. Here was someone he had business with, someone who was a damn sight more pleasant to look at than the grubby one-eyed bartender or the filth-caked nezumi at the far table.

Kiku stood in the doorway for a few seconds, sneering in disgust at the interior and everyone in it. She was stunningly beautiful and resplendently dressed, wrapped in pale purple silk and fine embroidered satin. Her wrap was slit up each side below her waist, revealing her shapely legs up to her hips, and her blouse was tightly wound around her to display both her considerable curves and her natural grace as she walked. She sported wide, flaring sleeves that ended just below the elbow and matching purple gauntlets that covered her forearms to the backs of her hands. Her bright black eyes glittered like precious stones, but the rest of her face was concealed behind a folded paper fan she used to waft the foul tavern air away from her face. A large purple camellia decorated Kiku's shoulder, its soft petals a perfect contrast to her sharp eyes and painted fingernails. Toshi thought her poise and beauty would have stood out at a rich man's formal banquet, but here in the Nest she was like a beautiful dream of an angel bringing him water in the desert.

Toshi sipped his drink to hide another smile. An angel, to be sure, but a dangerous one who could kill just about everyone in the room in one fell swoop if she cared to. Kiku was a *jushi*, a mage for hire who specialized in dark magic that was as powerful as it was unpleasant. Toshi had worked with Kiku before, so he was respectful but not afraid. He had convinced her to meet him here precisely because she was so formidable.

Kiku visibly steeled herself and strode boldly into the tavern. Wisely, none of the other patrons attempted to speak to her or catch her eye on the way. She stood next to Toshi for a moment, spread a purple satin square on the moldering old stool, and rested lightly on the edge of it.

"There's been a change in plans," she said. She snapped her fan shut and rested it across her lap. "Boss Uramon wants to see you now."

Toshi smiled foolishly. He toasted Kiku and spilled some of his drink on the bar. "That's not a problem. I want to see her, too."

Kiku reopened her fan with a loud crack, quickly enough that the metal spine at the edge shattered the tiny ceramic cup in Toshi's hand.

"You can drop the clumsy drunk act," she said. "I know you're neither."

Toshi glanced at his empty hand, his fingers still curled around the space where the cup had been. "All right," he said. "I was only doing it to spare the bartender's feelings." He leaned in and whispered, "He's very sensitive about the wine. I think his mother grows the rice herself."

Kiku sniffed. "She grows it in the septic fields, from the smell. Come on." She stood and motioned for Toshi to follow.

Toshi rose to his feet and tossed a few coins onto the bar. He had hoped for a chance to talk to Kiku alone about Uramon, but if the Boss wanted to see him sooner, he could accommodate that. Uramon was one of the most influential figures in the Takenuma underworld, and Toshi had worked for her in the past. It had taken some doing, but he had managed to redeem his contract with the Boss so that he was no longer obliged to serve her while also maintaining a cordial relationship with her. If she wanted to see him now, she either had work-for-hire or she wanted information.

In any case, all Toshi wanted now was to get inside Uramon's manor and take a look around. His discussion with Kiku could wait.

The purple-clad jushi held the door to let Toshi through first. He bobbed his head and stepped out onto the sodden bamboo deck.

"Oh," he said, when he saw the group waiting for him outside. "Great."

Six serious men armed with daggers and hatchets stood at the far end of the deck. Two more masked jushi waited next to a huge brindle dog with an enormous square head. The dog was silent, but he was straining so hard against his leash that his handler had to anchor himself onto one of the bamboo spires that held up the roof.

Before he could dash back into the bar or draw his sword, Toshi felt a gentle hand touch his shoulder. He tried to spin out from under the caress, but as he did he saw a flash of purple. He froze in mid-spin with one eye on the dog and the other on Kiku.

The jushi had placed one of her purple camellias on Toshi's shoulder. She was smiling casually.

"Don't worry," she said. "It won't do anything to you unless I tell it to."

Toshi remained rock-still, sweat beading across his forehead. Kiku's flowers could be deadlier than a snake bite and more caustic than acid.

"How do I keep you from telling it to?"

"By coming along peacefully. None of your tricks, none of your traps, none of your kanji magic. Uramon just wants to talk to you."

"I'm willing to talk. You don't need this. Or them." He motioned toward the hatchet men with his head.

"Self-obsessed, as usual." Kiku opened her fan and casually waved it under her chin. "This little outing was originally sent to bring back some troublesome rats who have been shockingly bold over the past few weeks. Uramon suspects someone new is moving in on her territory. Just as I was getting ready to come and see you, she requested the pleasure of your company. She said the other rats could wait."

"If there is someone moving in, it's not me. I've been lying low."

"I actually believe you. But it's not me you have to convince." She snapped the fan shut and prodded Toshi with it. "Move along now. Stay beside me and don't go to quickly. If I lose sight of you, the flower will put down roots in your torso."

"Thanks for the warning." Toshi glanced around at the

assembled mercenaries and goons as the hatchet men formed up around him. The two jushi and the dog took up the rear. Sadly, the friendliest face he saw belonged to the burly canine straining to break its leash and savage him.

"All right," he said. He gallantly offered his arm to Kiku. "Off we go."

Kiku sniffed and slapped his arm away with her fan.

* * * * *

Boss Uramon's manor was at the far end of the swamp on the border between Takenuma the ruins at the edge of Konda's domain. Her home had once belonged to a rich retainer, but he had been called away years ago to fight kami. When he didn't return, Uramon had his family and servants driven off so that she could move in. From here she kept an eye on her interests in the swamp as well as those in more polite society.

Dozens of low-level thugs meandered around the grounds as Kiku and Toshi led the strange procession through the main gate. Uramon employed a huge staff of indentured servants and outright slaves who had mortgaged their futures past the point of redemption. Her home was one of the busiest commerce centers in all Kamigawa, with a steady flow of black market goods and dozens of enterprising tradespeople looking for work. Uramon stood at the center of this network of illegal commerce, extracting her share of whatever goods or services passed through her hidden sphere influence.

Toshi knew the house well. For a time in his youth, he had been one of Uramon's reckoners, the brutal gangs that maintained her reputation through intimidation and violence. When someone defaulted on a usurious loan or failed to produce protection money, her reckoners paid a visit. When an Uramon courier was waylaid or some of her stolen property went missing, she sent her reckoners. Any debt, any slight, any injury to Uramon's organization would prompt a visit from the fallen warriors in her service.

It was a dirty, dangerous job, and getting out from under Uramon's influence was the best thing Toshi had ever done for himself. Years ago he had formed his own independent band of reckoners and dubbed them the hyozan. With a significant investment of time, effort, and currency, he had convinced Uramon to accept his departure. Now he was back, and while he had settled his account with Uramon, the Boss was never one to let go easily of something she owned. If he were lucky, she would merely ask him a few questions and offer him work. If not, things could get messy.

They left the dog and the hatchet men outside. The other jushi entered the manor but fell back and let Kiku lead him into the manor's interior. She stayed close as they went inside, brushing aside the sentries who rose to meet them. Since their party was expected, they had no trouble navigating through the opulent rooms on the first floor and climbing the staircase to Uramon's chamber on the second. The burly guards outside Uramon's room nodded to Kiku and opened the door.

Uramon kneeled in the center of the room. She was resting on a square stone platform in the middle of a rectangular pit filled with black sand. A collection of irregular-shaped rocks were scattered across the surface of the sand. Tall candles burned at each corner of the pit. Uramon carried a long-handled wooden rake, which she pulled through the sand, tracing parallel lines between and around the stones. She was singing softly to herself in a low, meditative voice, a study in tranquility.

Toshi had never been able to calculate Uramon's age. Her face was always covered in a thick layer of white powder, and her hair was either dyed black or she wore an excellent wig. She had a round face, but there was no softness to it. Her expression was always one of disinterest and her eyes were frequently half-closed. Behind her slitted lids, though, they were sharp and penetrating. Neither beautiful nor homely, Uramon's face was a nondescript mask that she had spent a lifetime perfecting. Unless she spoke or made eye contact, it was impossible to imagine how such a bland woman had mustered such a successful criminal empire. People taken in by this false lack of charisma often found themselves working for Uramon without knowing exactly how.

"Hail Uramon, venerable boss of Takenuma." Toshi bowed.

Uramon kept singing, but she lifted the rake out of the sand. Carefully, she hauled in the tool and rested it on the stone platform. Only then did she fall silent and gaze up at Toshi and Kiku.

"Umezawa," she said. "What a happy occasion this is. Thank you for coming."

Her voice was like her face, dull and unobtrusive, but Toshi did not relax. He knew the speed and the sharpness of the mind behind that sallow voice. Uramon would not be disarmed by his personality, so he must not be disarmed by hers.

"All you had to do was ask. We're old friends." He gestured to the camellia on his shoulder. "Now that I'm here, can we transplant Kiku's friend somewhere else?"

Uramon rose. "I think not. At least, not yet." She folded her arms into the sleeves of her simple black robe and stepped into her wooden sandals. As Toshi watched and waited, she shuffled across the surface of the black sand, barely disrupting the careful rake-lines and avoiding the stones. When she reached the edge of the pit and stepped onto the lacquered wooden floor, not a single grain of sand came with her.

She gestured for Toshi and Kiku to follow her as she crossed to the far side of the room. She sat on a square pillow facing the door and motioned for Toshi to step forward.

"I understand you've had some trouble with the *soratami*," she said.

"Moonfolk?" Toshi said. "I think I saw one once, as a boy, but they don't usually come to Numai."

"They don't usually come to any part of the swamp," Uramon said. "Lately, that has changed. I had hoped you would know something about it."

"No, Boss. I've been out of circulation ever since I got religion."

Uramon smiled indulgently. "It's good to pray, my boy. Although there's hardly a kami left who won't try to take a bite out of anyone who calls for its blessing."

"I'm new to it," Toshi admitted. "I don't think I've gotten the spirits' attention properly just yet, but I keep trying."

"Excellent. And you have no idea why the soratami have been stirring up the rats?"

"Have they? No, Boss, I don't."

"Hmm. That's not what Marrow-Gnawer told me."

Toshi forced a smile. "How is my old friend Marrow? I haven't seen him lately, either. Is he well?"

"Not at present, but he is very truthful. My hatchet men are experts at teasing the truth out of people, as I'm sure you recall."

Toshi's smile wavered. "Indeed I do. And he says I'm mixed up with the soratami? That's very odd. He's not very bright, you know. Perhaps he meant someone else?"

"Why don't we ask him together?" Uramon clapped her hands. The door to the chamber opened, and two large men dragged in a limp nezumi. The rat-man's feet barely scraped the floor.

"Open his eyes," Uramon said. One of the guards grabbed the black fur on top of Marrow-Gnawer's head, pulled his head back, and shook it.

Toshi held his frozen smile. One of Marrow's eyes was swollen shut, and his face was a mass of bloody bruises and badly healed cuts. Toshi glanced down and noticed two of his fingers were missing and that his legs were covered in tiny wounds like pinpricks.

Marrow-Gnawer groaned. His good eye fluttered open just as the second sentry tossed a dipper of water in his face.

The nezumi coughed and ran his long tongue across his lips and muzzle, taking up as much of the cool liquid as he could. The guard shook him again and shoved him forward so that he fell to his knees.

"Marrow-Gnawer," Uramon said. The rat-man hissed piteously.

The boss turned to Toshi. "He and his fellows were leaving one of my establishments with all of the night's revenue on their backs. Fortunately, my employees were able to convince the gang to stay and chat for a while. He told me quite a tale."

She spoke once more to the nezumi. "Tell Toshi what you told me, Marrow."

The rat-man groaned. He steadied himself on all fours and looked up at the humans. He coughed and wiped his mouth, leaving a streak of blood on the back of his hand.

"Moonfolk commissioned jobs in the ruins," he said. "Toshi interfered. Saw the soratami, ran off. But the job was ruined. The soratami blamed us, and now they own me and my whole tribe." He cast his eyes down again. "Didn't want to rob you, Boss. Had to. Soratami would have killed me."

"I understand, Marrow, but by now you must realize how short-sighted that decision was." Uramon nodded to the sentries, who hauled Marrow-Gnawer off his feet and dragged him into the corner of the room.

"So," she said. "The soratami are encroaching on my business. I would normally send my own reckoners to deal with this, but it seems that you already have an inside line on what they're up to."

"I don't, Boss. I really don't. It was bad luck that put me in the middle of Marrow's job. I just wanted to get away."

"I believe you, Toshi. Of course I do. But the facts as I see them are: The soratami are interfering with my operation, and they're using the nezumi as stooges. You've had dealings with both, and you were always one of my most reliable reckoners, in spite of your foolish insistence on freelancing."

Toshi tried to follow Uramon's lead and keep his voice neutral. "You want me to take on the moonfolk? I'm flattered, Boss, but I'm not qualified."

"Not on your own. With Kiku and a few of my hatchet men to back you up, you would have a much better chance. Especially if Marrow here brings you to his next meeting with the soratami so you have the element of surprise."

Uramon rose, stepped forward, and fixed her heavy-lidded eyes on Toshi. "I am commissioning you and your hyozan for a reckoning, boy. The soratami stole from me. They've been stealing from me for weeks. Take whatever and whomever you need to Marrow's next meeting. Kill as many of them as you can, and bring their heads back to me."

Toshi held the drab woman's gaze. "Too risky, Boss. Half the people you send won't make it back. I don't like those odds."

"I'm already sharing the risk, as are Kiku and her clan. But if it's compensation you're worried about, we can come to an arrangement."

Toshi shook his head. "Sorry, Boss. I refuse."

Uramon lashed out, striking Toshi across the face with the back of her hand. The black enameled ring on her little finger gouged a line of flesh from his cheek.

"You presume too much, Toshi. You may not refuse, because I want this. Your odds against the soratami are far better than your chances against Kiku's flower, and you will wear her bloom like a schoolgirl's corsage until you return to me with the goods in hand."

Boss Uramon turned. Her voice was soft and lifeless. "Take them out and clean them up. Kiku, my dear, I expect nothing short of brilliance from you. Toshi is a tricky one, but I have every confidence that you can keep him under control."

Toshi wiped the drops of blood from his cheek and glanced at Kiku. He hid a smile behind his hand as he stared at the ring on Uramon's hand. She didn't always wear it, but now that he knew she still possessed it he was free to take his leave.

"Don't do it," Kiku whispered. "Whatever you're thinking, don't do it."

"I don't have to do anything," Toshi said loudly. "If you kill me, you'll have the entire hyozan after you until my death is avenged. Your reckoners take revenge for you, Boss, to protect your business. Mine only work for each other."

"Who said anything about killing?" Uramon cocked her head and folded her hands into her sleeves. "I asked Kiku to plant a camellia not to make you dead but to make you wish you were dead. The reckoner oath you amateurs swore only applies if you're killed, am I right? Blind, dismembered, and in constant agony won't count."

The flower on his shoulder squirmed. Toshi looked hard at Kiku.

"The Boss is right," Kiku said. "That's a very special flower. It will never stop doing terrible things to you, but it won't kill you. The ogre shaman and the others will never know."

Toshi nodded. "I see you have all the angles covered, Boss. As usual."

"Of course. Now. I want you to begin as soon as—"

"But you've overlooked one important thing this time."

"Oh? And what might that be?"

"I've found religion—and the kami I pray to is one of the few that still answers."

Uramon replied, but Toshi was concentrating too hard to listen. There were kami spirits for everything in the utsu-shiyo—storms, rivers, stones, swords, light. Even concepts such as justice and rage had patron spirits in the kakuriyo. Toshi had fallen in with the Myojin of Night's Reach, the major spirit of darkness and secrecy, which held sway wherever there was no light. He made very few demands on her and she on him, but he had spent all of his time lately establishing what her power could do and how to invoke it. He was by no means expert, but he had learned to call upon her blessings in a manner that suited him perfectly.

The kanji carved into his arm months ago throbbed, invisible under his sleeve. Uramon was still talking, and he sensed Kiku shouting and waving her arms. The flower on his shoulder squirmed again, and the first painful points of its lethal roots pressed into his flesh.

Toshi disappeared under the probing tips of the plant, fading from sight like a wisp of steam. Invisible and intangible, he watched as the loathsome, wriggling bloom fell through the space he occupied and landed on the floor with a soft thud. He could still see and hear everything in the room as normal, but he could not be seen, or heard, or touched until the myojin's blessing wore off.

"Take that one back to his cell," snapped Uramon, gesturing at Marrow-Gnawer. She turned to Kiku and snarled softly, "I did not know Toshi was capable of such things."

"Nor I, Boss." Kiku scooped up the flower and closed her fist around it. When she opened her hand, the bloom was gone. "He kept saying he'd gotten religion, but he lies so often I barely listen to him anymore."

Uramon nodded, her slack face unchanged, her eyes hard and furious. "Gather your fellows and a dozen of my hatchet men. Search the grounds. He may have vanished, but he can't have gotten far. When you find him, bring him back here."

Still in the precise spot he had been, Toshi watched Kiku exit. Uramon was right—he was completely safe in this shroud of shadow, but he could not move quickly and could not stay concealed forever. As a phantom, he was too insubstantial to cast spells or cover great distances.

Fortunately, he didn't need to go far. With a colossal effort of will, Toshi floated after Uramon as the boss skirted the edge of her sand pit and exited the chamber.

Scott McGough

She still wore the ring, which was half of what he wanted
from her. If she didn't lead him to the other half soon, he would
strike out on his own and search the manor himself. So long as
the guards and Kiku were searching outside, it wouldn't even
matter when the myojin's blessing faded. By then, he meant to be
well on his way, safe with the information he came for.

CHAPTER 3

Solid and visible once more, Toshi trudged through the muck at the south end of the great Takenuma Swamp. He had learned all he needed to in Uramon's manor before slipping out and following the slow, tortuous route of a phantom to safety.

When Night's blessing finally left him, he was just outside Uramon's property. He knew someone in Uramon's employ would be able to track him—either the nezumi by scent or the jushi by spell. He moved on as quickly as he could, taking no special measures to hide his trail. Toshi had a gift for self-preservation and improvisation that had kept him alive and out of extreme poverty among the fen's cutthroat community. Uramon's interest in him changed the order of his long-term goals but not the goals themselves. Let them follow. He could actually use a gang of expendable thugs, provided he stayed one step ahead of them.

The ground slowly began to firm under his feet as he left the outskirts of the swamp and headed into the cold, rocky realm of the Sokenzan Mountains. Toshi saw the thin, needle-like spires that littered the horizon and tightened his cloak against the dry, chill air. He had traveled from the fen to the mountains and back a dozen times or more, but normally he was much farther east. His present heading took him along the western edge of the range, where the cold was more constant and the snow never melted but was driven into drifts by the bitter wind.

He had done far more than pray since his last trip to the mountains. There was a surprising amount of commerce between the fen and the Sokenzan, and his ability to go unnoticed permitted him unprecedented access to private conversations between bandits and black marketeers.

He collected quite a bit of useful information about the western quadrant of the range. Here was where the greatest concentration of akki goblins lived, tribes of a thousand or more dug into the frozen hills like bees in a hive. Here the great *sanzoku* bandit chieftain Godo had escaped the daimyo's troops time and again, raiding the great lord's riches then melting away into the rocky wastes. Here the spirits of stone and bloodlust roamed, as sharp and unforgiving as the landscape itself. Here were peaks blighted and accursed, haunted by wild spirits more terrible than anything society had encountered—even the twisted and corrupt society of the swamp.

Toshi wasn't sure how much of this was truth and how much was sanzoku bragging, but he was sure that the next step in his spiritual evolution waited for him at the top of one of these frozen spits of rock.

He plowed on through the dusty, ankle-deep snow for the better part of a day. The farther south he went, the colder it got. At last, he reached the foothills of the western Sokenzan and saw his path rising up before him, a long, treacherous way that disappeared into the mist and low-lying clouds above.

He had memorized the only maps of this region, so he was able to identify the mountain he wanted. The akki and bandits called it the Heart of Frost and they avoided it at all costs. Toshi grinned, hoping that whoever was following him on Uramon's behalf did not share the superstition.

He glanced back through the swirling snow. He could not see anyone in the distance, but he knew they were there. He had backtracked just before he left the swamp, careful not to be seen but ready to invoke his myojin if necessary. Sure enough, there were a half-dozen nezumi and several humans struggling to keep up with him. They kept Marrow-Gnawer on a leash, forcing him to keep his nose buried in the muck so as not to lose Toshi's trail.

They were only a few hours behind, which suited him perfectly. Once up on the mountainside, he could stand aside, let them take the lead, and see if the stories about the Heart of Frost were true.

The wind changed direction, and for a moment Toshi was at the calm center of a whirling vortex of wind and snow. He felt a tingling on his skin that had nothing to do with the cold and a dull pressure on his eardrums.

"Muck and mire," he swore. He didn't have time for this.

The air continued to swirl around him as a huge, amorphous shape formed overhead. These were all the signs of a kami manifestation, of a spirit completing the journey from the kakuriyo to the utsushiyo. Once a random occurrence like a flood or a lightning strike, these intrusions had become more frequent and more violent over the past two decades until the conclusion was inescapable: the kami had declared war on the material world.

Once the spirits were draped in flesh, they were vulnerable to physical attacks, but they were savage, focused, and powerful enough to pose a real danger to anyone they encountered. Toshi had battled several kami during his life, but his experience did not shore up his confidence. He preferred to keep clear of such encounters altogether, especially when he was being pursued.

The form in the air reminded him of some great misshapen bird, half-obscured by the driving snow so that he could barely determine its outline. It had broad wings that didn't move, four clawed feet, and a long stinging tail. He could see no head, but its eyes glowed yellow in the space where a head might be. A flock of hovering blue fish as thin as needles hovered in the cold, whirling wind around the creature. It let out a grating shriek, turned, and sliced toward Toshi like a thrown blade.

The ochimusha dived aside and rolled through the snow. Whatever it was, it was fast. He glanced at the ground where he had been standing and saw a clean, precise furrow that the kami had cut into the ground. If he had been a little slower, he would have been in pieces.

Toshi cursed his luck. He had made his reputation as a kanji mage, but his recent conversion to kami worship required him to relearn some of his most basic maneuvers. A year ago, he could have dispatched the snow kami in minutes with his swords and the right character. A year from today, the blessings of Night would stop the spirit bird in mid-flight. Right now, however, he had to figure out a way to blend both together before the hostile kami split him down the middle.

The kami made another pass, which he narrowly avoided. Toshi drew his swords and crossed them in front of him, turning to keep them between himself and the kami. If it were mindless enough, it might shred itself against his blades on its next strike.

The wind redoubled, and the flying kami became a blur. Toshi felt a shock and heard a metallic crack as the spirit slammed into his crossed blades. Thrown back by the impact, Toshi lost his long blade when his back met a large boulder alongside the path.

His vision doubled, and he shook his head to clear it. The kami darted like a dragonfly, dashing to Toshi's left and right so quickly he could scarcely follow its motion. He was safer with his back to the boulder, but the loss of his sword balanced that advantage. He felt a warm liquid running down the back of his empty hand. The spirit's sharp body had split open the flesh between his knuckles, and blood dripped down onto the frozen ground.

Reflexively, Toshi tried to come up with an appropriate kanji symbol he could inscribe using his own blood—a kanji inscribed with bodily humors was far more powerful than one done in ink or chalk. The bird moved too fast for him to mark it, but maybe he could mark something else.

With his short sword held out in one hand, Toshi kept his eyes fixed on the slashing kami and probed the rock behind him with his bleeding fist. He quickly traced the kanji that had allowed him to escape Uramon and Kiku, the first spell he had cast after accepting the blessings of Night's Reach. Normally, it was a straightforward concealment charm. With the power of the myojin behind it, it was something far more profound.

The wind-shear kami came screaming forward, its wings spread wide. Toshi focused his thoughts and felt the sting of the myojin-powered mark on his forearm.

"Fade," he said, rapping his bloody fist on the rock behind him. He pressed his palm flat against the center of the character he'd inscribed.

The kami came on, gathering speed. Toshi felt his body melt away. He lowered his sword.

The scything air spirit soared through him without resistance and on into the now- insubstantial boulder. It banked and tried to come up short of the mountainside beyond the phantom stone.

Toshi concentrated on his palm and the kanji beneath it. He felt the point of contact between his body, the symbol, and the stone, then stepped away.

The surface of the rock clung to his palm for a moment then peeled off. Robbed of its living energy, the kanji spell winked out like a candle between moistened fingertips. The boulder became solid once more—Toshi could see the wind-driven snow change course as the mass of stone returned to deflect it.

Trapped inside, the wind-shear kami found its body irrevocably woven into the rock. Only the tips of its wings and its glowing eyes protruded. Its last shrieking cry slowly lost strength and volume until it died against the wind in Toshi's ears.

He stood and watched until the spirit's form had shimmered and vanished from sight. They always evaporated after they died. In the growing storm, he could see strange patterns in the surface of the rock where the kami's wings had poked through.

Toshi retrieved his sword. He bandaged his hand, tightened his pack, and started up the mountain trail.

From here on in, he knew, things were going to get tricky.

CHAPTER 4

They had been climbing for three days. Toshi's trail mean-dered but never strayed far from the path thawing snow had carved into the Heart of Frost. It was a monotonous and exhaust-ing enterprise, made all the more so by the nezumi trackers and the hatchet men.

As a professional Kiku was obliged to retrieve Toshi. The others were merely slaves or prisoners, pathetically trying to cling onto their lives before Uramon took them completely. The jushi swore to make Toshi pay. She had known him for years, had worked with him when he was one of Uramon's reckoners. They had never come into professional conflict, so they had managed not to make any serious attempts on each other's lives until now.

A nezumi stopped on the path in front of her to sniff the air. Without slowing or breaking stride, Kiku kicked the rat-man aside and kept trudging through the snow.

He squawked and growled, "Hey! How am I—"

Kiku turned and glared. The craven little vermin suddenly curled himself into a ball and covered his face, mewling pite-ously. Kiku pulled her heavy hooded cloak tight and cursed the ochimusha once more.

She would kill Toshi for this. She hated the cold, she hated nezumi, and she hated owing Boss Uramon. If Toshi had just knuckled under and agreed to do the job, things would have been perfect. Uramon would have sent them out to ambush the soratami, and they'd have been obliged to deliver. Apart from that, whatever arrangement she and Toshi came to once the job was underway would have been entirely up to them. She did not trust him, but she did like the idea of putting his skills and his devious mind to work for her benefit.

The wind cut through her clothes, and she grimaced. Look at us now, she thought. You're running to the least hospitable place in the world in the hopes it'll keep us from following you, and I have to bring you back. There's no chance of any side deals or limited partnership now, Toshi Umezawa. I'm readying another very special flower just for you.

Soon there wouldn't be enough light to continue. The nezumi could track at night, but the temperature on the mountain dropped dangerously low in the dark. If they didn't take shelter they'd be dead in a matter of hours.

Kiku stopped. "Marrow-Gnawer," she said, "come here."

Marrow-Gnawer growled something at his fellow rats and skittered back down the path. He was wearing a leather collar that fit tightly around his neck.

"How far ahead is he?"

Marrow-Gnawer grunted. "Half a day or less. Hard to tell in the cold."

Kiku pulled out her fan and snapped it open. She used it to cover her face from the eyes down and leaned down to Marrow-Gnawer.

"Send two of your friends ahead. Have them go as far as they can. If they catch sight of him, they can come back and tell us."

Marrow-Gnawer glared, but his voice was calm. "Excuse, ma'am. They'll die before dawn."

Kiku leaned closer, the fan undulating slightly. "I don't care. If he's close enough to catch, I want to know tonight."

Marrow-Gnawer nodded, his face grim. "Even if they see him, they'll die. Why not just kill them here?" He put his hand on the jagged rusty blade on his hip. "Or let me."

Kiku stood up. "I have a feeling—" she waved her fan more vigorously—"that he's closer than you think. It'd be like him to double back and spring something on us."

She snapped the fan shut and smiled at the nezumi leader. "Send two up the path, now. Or I'll send the whole lot of you, one in every direction."

Marrow-Gnawer nodded. "Yes, ma'am."

* * * * *

Marrow's scouts came back just before dawn. Kiku was awake and ready when he cleared his throat outside her tent.

"What have they found?"

"A symbol," Marrow-Gnawer replied. "A kanji painted on the bark of a tree."

Kiku stepped out into the frigid night. The snow and wind had stopped, and the stars were clear and brittle overhead. Kiku's breath came in thick white clouds through the scarf covering her face.

"Painted with what?"

Marrow-Gnawer looked pained. "Didn't say."

Kiku rolled her eyes. "Too much to suppose you illiterate dungballs recognized the symbol?"

Marrow-Gnawer shook his head. "No, jushi. Not nezumi-tongue."

Kiku muttered and then turned to the camp behind her. "Get ready to move out." She stepped forward to Marrow-Gnawer. "Stay close. I want you to show me the symbol as quickly as possible."

Under her withering gaze, the rest of the party began to break camp. Within a few minutes, one of Uramon's hatchet men came running.

"What is it?"

The man was large and gruff, but his bluster had been dulled by living wild. "You'd better come see this, ma'am."

He led her off the path and onto a patch of frozen scrub. He worked his way around the largest clump of brambles then stepped back,

Kiku came around the bush. She stared silently at the base of the brambles, her frosty breath flowing in a single thin stream.

Two of the hatchet men lay dead, flat on their backs, wearing expressions of wide-eyed horror. Their mouths were open. Their faces were blue. Their hair and beards were thick with ice crystals.

Each was fully dressed but disheveled, as if they had thrown their clothes on in a hurry. Kiku stretched forward and tapped her closed fan on the nearest dead man's eye. The metal spine clinked against the frozen orb.

Kiku tapped her fan along the man's brow, down his nose, across his lips, and under his chin. She nodded.

"Solid as a rock," she said. She turned to where the ashen-faced thug stood, nervously thumbing the hatchet on his belt. "If you hit him with a rock, he'll shatter.

"Come on," she said. "I need to see this symbol the rats found."

The party packed up the camp and strapped their heavy loads to their backs. In silence they hiked behind the nezumi scouts and Marrow-Gnawer. To the rear, the rest of the nezumi pack and Uramon's thugs scanned both sides of the path, fearful as children.

Kiku herself kept her eyes on the path ahead. The fact that something had lured the dead men out of their tents bothered her. She'd have been more comfortable if Toshi had just murdered them in their sleep.

The sun was clear of the horizon by the time they reached the symbol. Marrow-Gnawer's brethren chittered and gestured excitedly, skittering around the base of the trunk. He grabbed them each by the shoulder and hauled them aside as Kiku marched up to the tree.

She stared at the symbol, shaking her head in disbelief. Toshi truly was mad. The Heart of Frost was already cursed, and he decides to make *this* symbol, in his own blood, no less, on one of the only living things hearty enough to survive this killing cold.

"Ma'am," one of the hatchet men called. "What's it mean?"

She looked from one face to another, from Uramon's grizzled and scarred disasters to the hairy, cunning animals in Marrow-Gnawer's group. Was it worth telling them what Toshi had unleashed? Was it important for them to know that they were all a half-breath away from doom, Toshi included?

They might run. Not that it would do them any good, but they might run.

She could run. She could go back and tell Uramon that her

incompetent servants all got themselves killed by one of Toshi's traps. The boss would believe that. She would have a lower opinion of Kiku, and her jushi clan would have to make good on the failure, but Kiku would be alive.

"Where's Uchida?" another thug said. Kiku cocked her head at the hatchet man who spoke.

"Who?" she said.

"Uchida. The one who found the bodies this morning. He was bringing up the rear, but he's not there anymore."

Kiku snarled. To Marrow-Gnawer, she said, "Backtrack the way we came. You'll probably find him just off the path. When you do, get back here as fast as you can."

Marrow nodded and made a barking noise in his throat. Two more nezumi barked back, and the three scrabbled back down the mountain, disappearing over a ridge.

The hatchet man who had asked about the kanji stepped up. "Ma'am," he said. "What's going on?"

Kiku ignored him.

Marrow-Gnawer and his partners soon returned. They were panting and raised huge clouds of white mist in the air around them. The others fell to their knees in the snow, but Marrow-Gnawer simply rested his hands on his knees.

"Dead," he husked. "Hundred yards or so back."

Kiku nodded. "Frozen, like the others."

"Yeh."

"How's that possible?" one of the hatchet men called.

"Yeh, the sun's up," echoed a nezumi.

Kiku eyes flared. With a curse, she drew her fan and knocked Marrow-Gnawer off his feet with a wide backhand stroke.

"You feeble, pox-ridden vermin," she growled. "This can't be the first kanji Toshi has made like this. He's probably been bleeding on rocks and patches of ice all the way up the mountain. This is just the first one you worthless blobs have seen."

Marrow-Gnawer bared his horrible, jagged teeth and spat blood from his mouth. He scrabbled up on all fours and said, "What, then? What did we miss? What is it?"

Kiku paused, glaring back down the path. It was behind them now as well as in front. There was no point in running now. Alone, she'd be just another easy target. Among the rabble Uramon had saddled her with . . . she was the only wolf in a herd of sheep. As such, she might be able to surprise the other wolf who'd come to make a kill.

Kiku offered her closed fan to Marrow-Gnawer. The nezumi hesitated then grabbed the end. Kiku pulled forward, lifting Marrow to his feet.

"We need to stick together now," she said. "We're in *her* territory. I don't know if Toshi summoned her here or if she was already here and he just stirred her up—but this is her mountain, and we can't get off it without facing her."

"Her," Marrow-Gnawer echoed. "Who—what—is 'her'?"

Kiku shook her head. "Not now. We've got to save our breath and keep moving. If we can catch Toshi before nightfall, we have a much better chance of seeing another sunrise."

Kiku marched up the path toward the summit of the mountain without waiting for the trackers to pick up Toshi's trail. There was only one way to go anymore, and she meant to go as quickly as she could.

She wrapped her cloak around herself and lowered her hood to shield her eyes from the rising sun. Behind Kiku, the others murmured and wondered and prayed as they struggled to pick up their packs and keep pace with her. Marrow-Gnawer was the first to fall in step just behind her, but the others were quick to join the line.

No one wanted to be left alone on the path, not even in broad daylight.

* * * * *

"The creature is called *yuki-onna*," Kiku said. "The Snow Woman."

Marrow-Gnawer and several of the hatchet men groaned. They had come a long distance in the short hours daylight allotted them. There had been no sign of Toshi at all. His trail and his scent had vanished completely just as the sun began to dip over the Sokenzan Range.

They all sat round the biggest campfire they could build, crouching in a rocky hollow that protected them from the rising wind. They had given up asking Kiku questions early in the hike, so they were surprised when she suddenly began to talk.

The jushi stared at the fire as she spoke. Her voice had a practiced quality to it, as if she were reciting facts learned long ago. Kiku had learned much from her clan elders, but none of them had faced what she was now facing. All she had to go on were second-hand accounts and ancient folktales, and none of them were encouraging.

"There are stories about woodcutters and lonely ferrymen who die in the bitter cold among the ice and snow. These are not city folk who are unaccustomed to bad weather but men who have lived through score of winters, outdoorsmen who respect the power of the cold. They know how to survive, and better, they know when it's not safe to go outside.

"These same men are found outdoors, nonetheless, frozen stiff a short walk from their homes and their beds. Sometimes they die in bed with a roaring fire not five feet away, frosted white and cold as if they had been left naked on a field of ice."

"How is that possible?"

Kiku did not look away from the flame. "It is not the weather that kills them. It is the yuki-onna. She comes to them in the form of a beautiful woman or a loved one. She lures them out of their homes, away from their stew pots and wool blankets, out into the night. She calls them, and they answer, following her until they can walk no more. If they are safely asleep indoors, she enters, appearing as a dream. She enters in the guise of someone they love or someone they could have loved. She approaches them, though her feet never touch the ground.

"Indoors or out, she goes to them. She caresses their faces or kisses their lips, but her touch is cold . . . no, more than just cold. Much more. She is a primordial force of nature, a consumer of warmth and devourer of life. One embrace and the victim's body becomes a solid block of ice."

Kiku continued to stare at the fire as her words soaked in. The wind rose, blowing smoke and embers past her face.

Marrow-Gnawer coughed. "What do we do?" he said. "How do we not die?"

"I don't know. But none of us can ever be alone from now on. It's much harder for her to snare more than one at a time."

A hatchet man grunted anxiously. "We're still not safe. She got the first two, and they were together."

Kiku flicked her eyes at the speaker. "I didn't say safe. I said safer."

"For how long?" The man was starting to panic. "If we're doomed anyway, what's the point in waiting? Let's go find this thing and hack it up."

A few of the others muttered in support. Kiku was silent.

After a few moments, the hatchet man said, "I mean, we *can* fight her, can't we?"

"I've never heard of anyone who has," Kiku said. "Before you go rushing out into the dark to die, think on this. Toshi made this happen. The kanji he made are somehow influencing her, steering her toward us. She can be affected by magic." Kiku stood, tossing open her cloak to reveal the purple flower pinned to her shoulder. "And I've got lots of that.

"Besides, it's also possible that killing Toshi will undo what he's done. All we have to do is catch him and put his head in a bag. If the yuki-onna comes for us after that, we can throw it at her."

"Will that help?"

Kiku grinned, her sharp eyes glittering in the firelight. "It can't hurt."

* * * * *

Kiku took the first watch, but she didn't trust the others to keep her alive, so she stayed awake as long as she could. Their plan was as solid as it could be, considering the circumstances. It had to be simple enough for the nezumi to follow, and it had to keep them clustered together as closely and for as long as possible during the night.

They ringed their tents in a tight circle with the entrances facing inward. The sentries were tied together at the leg and tied again to the individual tents. If they saw anyone or heard anything, they were to make as much noise as possible so the others could prevent them from wandering off in the dark. If the sentries wandered off anyway, they would drag one of the tents with them and thus raise the alarm. If a black-eyed woman in flowing white robes appeared on the edge of camp, they were to attack her with whatever weapons they had, as loudly as possible.

Kiku kept her tent flap half-open. She closed her eyes for what seemed like the briefest of moments, but when she woke the sun was rising.

Three of the nezumi had frozen to death in their tents. Their hairy black bodies were covered in a thick dusting of ice and their frozen whiskers broke off when their brethren tried to rouse them. The survivors silently buried the dead in a mound of snow.

As the others packed up for the day's hike, Kiku calculated. Three hatchet men and three nezumi left, plus her. For the first time in her life, Kiku wished there were more rats around.

The real flaw in Toshi's gambit struck her. He had set the yuki-onna on them, but he himself was still atop the Heart of Frost. Unless he was practicing some epic magic, there was no way to prevent the yuki-onna from coming after him once the others were gone. This was not a myojin to be appeased with prayers but a primordial spirit with the cruel instincts of a predator. As far as the jushi knew, a yuki-onna could not be stopped, only distracted by easier prey. What would Toshi do when there were no more distractions? The snow woman would come for him before he had descended the mountain even halfway.

Hope flared in Kiku's mind, the savage realization that she was not doomed if she could just puzzle out the problem before her. Toshi had called something unstoppably lethal down upon them all, something he would not have done if he didn't have a trick in store that would allow him to survive. She doubted his disappearing act would save him—the snow woman fed on the spirit as much as the body, and as long as Toshi was alive he was vulnerable. What was his angle? What did he know that she didn't?

"Ma'am!" Marrow-Gnawer's gruff voice fairly squeaked with excitement as he bustled up.

Kiku straightened her cloak. "What is it?"

"We've found Toshi. His scent. He's less than a few hundred yards up the path." Marrow-Gnawer gestured. "We should go now, catch him quick."

"For once, little vermin, we agree. Drop your pack and tell your brothers to do the same. Find Toshi and keep him in sight, but do not let him see you. Follow him wherever he goes, and make sure you leave a trail we can follow. When he stops—and he will—wait for us. I want to personally make him tell us the way out of this." Kiku opened her cloak and sniffed her camellia. "I'm looking forward to that."

Marrow-Gnawer shuddered. "Yes, ma'am." He shucked his pack and scurried off to collect the other nezumi. Within moments, the three were moving up the path at top speed.

Kiku waited until they were out of sight. She waved to the last three hatchet men, beckoning them closer.

When they were at arm's length, she said, "Drop your packs. We need to stay close behind the nezumi. Toshi wouldn't have let us pick up his trail if he didn't have something waiting for us."

The hatchet men chuckled. One said, "So we let them spring the trap, then we charge in and grab him."

Kiku nodded. "That's the plan. Besides, I'd rather let them die for the cause. Boss Uramon won't even miss them. She's indifferent to the fate of her cheapest slaves."

The hatchet men smiled at her. Kiku also smiled, but not for the same reason.

CHAPTER 5

Summoning the snow woman was not something Toshi wanted to make a habit of. She would have come for them on her own eventually—this was her mountain and she its curse. Every time he drew the symbol he felt her presence, with all its terrible gravity and endless cold. Leaving these special kanji in his wake was like tossing raw meat out to lure a hungry wolf. She was drawn to the symbols and the much larger group instead of poor Toshi, miserable and defenseless all by his lonesome.

He crouched now on a wide, flat shelf below a rocky point overlooking the path below. After making sure the nezumi would find him, he scaled the point to watch his game play out. He had spent most of the night setting the stage, and now he was ready to enjoy the show. The circular clearing below him was completely unremarkable, his efforts hidden under a light dusting of fresh snow. As he had with the wind shear kami at the base of the mountain, he had combined Night's blessings with the practical and reliable tools he knew best. He was eager to see how effective this mixture could be.

Something whirred in the cold morning sky and Toshi leaned back against the rock. He shielded his eyes from the rising sun and saw a fluttering figure descending toward him. He mistook it for a bird at first, but then he saw it was a messenger kanji—a simple spell for communicating across great distances.

Toshi drew his jitte. He knew precious few people who used messengers and he didn't want to hear from any of them. If the kanji didn't attack, he was ready to nullify it before it could return to its master and report his location.

The kanji messenger fluttered down like a butterfly. It was a crude job, drawn with heavy bold strokes, and it did not seem to have cutting edges. Neither was it moving fast enough to inflict damage. Toshi kept his jitte handy as the messenger oriented on his shelf and then hovered just a few yards away, bobbing and rotating in the air.

"Well?" Toshi said. "Get on with it."

The edges of the kanji began to vibrate. A dull, droning buzz rose, then a soft and throaty female voice said, "I have a new commission for him and his band of reckoners.

Toshi blinked. He recognized the voice, but he could not credit what it was saying. And when had the daimyo's daughter learned to work messenger kanji?

"I am in my father's tower. I am a prisoner. Rescue me, and his reward will stagger the greediest of hearts. Even his."

Toshi shook his head in disbelief and muttered, "She really must be desperate."

The kanji bobbed again, and Michiko's voice said, "I will be waiting for him."

The edges of the symbol began to flake away. A real beginner's effort, Toshi thought. It isn't going to wait for a reply or even return to its starting point. Michiko might as well have tied a note to a rock.

He had offered his services to Michiko-hime only to get them both out of a tight spot. He had thought she would keep him on retainer or just use him for information. In a pinch, she might have him spy on someone. She was too young and held no official offices for her to send him on missions that might endanger him. Now she wanted him to break her out of the most tightly guarded piece of property in Kamigawa.

Toshi sighted. This was the result of working with the noble classes. He thought about sending her a return messenger, but the only reply he could give her was, "I'm working on it." Best to let her sit tight until he could figure out how to handle this new challenge. Right now, he had enough to worry about.

Down below, he saw his old friend Marrow and two more nezumi creeping toward the edge of the kanji circle he'd made. Trust Kiku to send in a sacrifice first. It was a smart move, but Toshi was unconcerned. His plan would work even if the nezumi were the only ones to break the circle of kanji that waited beneath the snow.

The rats were cautious, though, sniffing around the edges of the broad, flat section of the path. A hundred years ago, before the mountain was cursed, this spot would have been a perfect place to pitch a tent and ride out a storm. Now the nezumi crawled through the snow with only the tips of their noses poking out. They left dull gray furrows in as they spread out in a slow, careful formation. Marrow was taking no chances.

Toshi watched them explore. They were very close to the circle now. Just a few more moments . . .

Something else moved on the distant path, and the nezumi stopped where they were. Toshi peered through the midday glare and saw people coming up the path. Three men trying to be cautious and unseen but failing miserably.

Kiku's second wave, obviously. The jushi wasn't taking any chances, either, in case Toshi's trap was powerful enough to keep killing after it had been triggered.

Smart girl, he thought. *Of course it is. Then again, I didn't tell you to follow me, did I? Each choice in life brings rewards and punishments. The choice to bring me back to Uramon just carries more of the latter.*

Marrow-Gnawer had turned and lifted his head out of the snow. Seeing the hatchet men, he hissed a warning and motioned for them to drop lower to the ground. The thugs resisted at first, unwilling to take orders from a rat. Then they remembered Marrow was far sneakier than they were and they'd do well to follow his lead. Clumsily, they crouched and began to creep forward.

Toshi was so intent on tracking Marrow's progress that he almost missed the sound. The soft scrape of a boot on frozen rock filtered through his brain. As he was beginning to wonder where Kiku was, he saw a flash of purple spinning gently toward him.

He barely got his short sword out in time to intercept the camellia. The delicate purple bloom fastened onto his weapon, green stems and brown roots wrapping tightly around the blade. Its subtle fragrance changed from perfume to poison in his nostrils and the flower bore down on him, pressing on the sword as if its weight had increased a thousand times. Toshi was forced back into the sheer rock behind him, all of the strength in his arms and legs now devoted to keeping the flower and its grasping tendrils away from his face.

Kiku pulled herself onto the shelf. Her cloak was tossed back, revealing one shapely silk-clad shoulder and another purple flower.

"Hello, Toshi," she said. Her eyes were hard and bright.

Toshi struggled to keep the flower from pressing his sword into his own face. "Hello, Kiku. I . . . wasn't expecting you. At least—" he grunted and took a step forward, but the flower pressed him back once more—"not this high up."

"Yet here I am." She casually sniffed the camellia on her shoulder and stepped to the edge of the shelf.

"I have him," she said. "Marrow-Gnawer and you—" she pointed at the smallest hatchet man—"come help get him down." She turned back to Toshi.

"You can call off the yuki-onna," she said, "or you die here. Personally, I want you to come back and beg Uramon for mercy. I'd like to see that." She smiled coldly.

Toshi sneered over his blade. "Can't . . . call her off. But maybe . . ."

He turned his wrists so the blade's edge bit into the camellia. The flower pressed on, slicing off a third of itself as it slid over the blade toward Toshi's face.

Toshi sidestepped the lunging bloom and drew his jitte from his belt. The long, spiked truncheon was normally a defensive weapon, suited for blocking incoming swords and catching them in the metal tine that rose up from its handle. As the camellia flew by his face, Toshi thrust the sharpened end of his jitte through the bottom of the flower, spiking it against the cliff face. He pivoted around the pinned flower then slung it off the end of his weapon like a stone from a sling.

The ruined flower smacked against Kiku's chest, but it did her no harm. Even if it weren't crushed, impaled, and in pieces, she was the gardener who'd grown it . . . it could no more harm her than a snake could suffer from its own venom.

Toshi suddenly winced as an icy, stabbing pain lanced through his forearm. He glanced down past Kiku to the clearing below.

"We should talk," Toshi said. He kept his sword and his jitte ready. "I think one of Uramon's hatchet-heads just stepped inside my circle."

The clouds overhead thickened, and a dense shadow fell over them all. Kiku's eyes narrowed. She spread her fan, took a step back, and looked down.

It was dark as dusk in the clearing. The nezumi were whining and mewling in terror, their beady red eyes darting around for an escape route. The hatchet men were slightly more composed but at least as frightened. Halfway up the wall to the shelf, Marrow-Gnawer and the third hatchet man had stopped and were staring down in horror. The thug on the wall below Marrow screamed.

A pale figure materialized from the gloom, small-boned and graceful. Her gleaming white robes dragged along the surface of the snow without disturbing it, and though she came steadily forward her legs did not move. Her head was tilted forward so that her long, lustrous black hair completely concealed her face as it hung almost to the ground.

The nezumi wailed. The hatchet men on the ground turned to run. Kiku glared at Toshi over the edge of her fan.

"You're a bastard, Toshi Umezawa, and you've killed us all."

Toshi grinned. He sheathed his sword but kept his jitte in his hand.

"Perhaps," he said, "but I think I can save one or two of us. Interested?"

The closest nezumi stood like a statue, rigid with fear as the yuki-onna approached. She extended a pale hand from beneath the cascade of hair and white robes. Shuddering, weeping, helpless, the nezumi could only stand and sputter as that gentle hand touched his face.

Even from the height of the rock shelf, Toshi heard the crackling as the rat-man's body froze. A patina of frost spread out from the yuki-onna's hand, crusting the nezumi's hair with crystals of ice.

The two fleeing hatchet men reached the far side of the clearing. Before they hurtled down the path, they both stopped and cried out.

The snow woman was there, having finished with the first nezumi, as if she were a hostess unwilling to let her guests go without a proper goodbye. She stood before them, her face still hidden beneath the shroud of hair, and reached out with both hands. She placed her palms tenderly, almost lovingly on each man's shoulder. The vapor from their exhalations fell in fine crystals like snow as their eyes clouded and the blood froze in their veins.

Kiku did not take her eyes off the dread creature. "I'm interested, Toshi. Tell me more."

The yuki-onna shimmered from sight then reappeared and claimed the second nezumi. The rat-man fell back and disappeared into a snowdrift. Below Toshi and Kiku, the last hatchet man yelled as he lost his footing and tumbled down to the ground.

"What do you know about kami worship?" Toshi said. "Quickly—she's running out of thugs to play with."

"I know a great deal . . . probably more than you. What are you getting at?"

Toshi pulled up his sleeve. "See this mark? It's a powerful kanji we professionals use to make subtle entrances and exits. I made this one under the blessing of a powerful myojin. It works much better than it ever has before, and it won't heal. I think it's permanent."

Below, the hatchet man hurled his weapon. The yuki-onna barely paused as the axe sailed through her.

Kiku shrugged. "So what?"

"So, I think it means something. You don't pray to the kami of fire when you want it to rain, right? But if you make the right prayer to the right spirit, you get a thing of beauty. Something you can really use. I asked Night to let me fade away, but she did much more. You think about how much happens in the dark, how much of our business is conducted but never seen. How many people come and go, how many major events occur unnoticed in the shadows? I think I tapped into something larger and deeper than a concealment spell. I think this kanji makes me formless, like a shadow. It doesn't make me invisible—it makes me not there."

Screaming in terror, the last hatchet man bolted up the path, heading for the summit of the Heart of Frost. He made it ten steps before the snow woman appeared in front of him.

Kiku opened her hand, revealing a fresh camellia. "This is an interesting theory. Even if I believe you've been blessed by the Myojin of Night's Reach, it doesn't explain why you're still talking. Do something, if you can."

Toshi slid his sleeve back down. "I already did."

Kiku nodded toward the rampaging yuki-onna. "Maybe you should tell her, because she hasn't noticed."

Marrow-Gnawer pulled himself up on to the shelf. Below, the final hatchet man fell dead in the snow.

"Please," the nezumi said. He fell to his knees and placed his hands on the shelf. "Don't let her get me."

Kiku made as if to kick Marrow's trembling form off the shelf, but Toshi stopped her with a raised hand.

"I harnessed . . . I became part of an essential aspect of the myojin. And she let me."

The snow woman looked up at the shelf. A stiff wind blew her black tresses away from her face. Marrow-Gnawer screamed.

Her eyes were vacant black pools, terrible holes that led to a vast frigid void. She opened her pale lips and let out a ghastly, shrieking cry that stabbed through Toshi's ears and made him wince.

She floated towards the wall that Marrow-Gnawer had just climbed.

Kiku grabbed Toshi's arm. "Get to the point, ochimusha."

"Shadow is an aspect of Night. So is cold . . . that frigid emptiness that forces people to huddle together during the winter." He pointed. "She embodies cold. Cold is part of night. With my myojin's help, I think we can bend the yuki-onna to our will. Because if you think about it, hers is just another aspect of my patron's power."

The snow woman floated up the side of the sheer rock wall. Kiku waved away Toshi's argument. "The snow woman is not a horse to be broken or a dog to be leashed. She is a force of nature."

"That she is. I don't even think she has a will to be broken. But I've proven she can be led. Now all we have to do is prove she can be compelled."

"Enough of this. By the stony gray hell, stop making speeches and *do* something."

"All right, but don't yell at me when you don't like it. Give me your hand. You too, Marrow."

The nezumi leapt to his feet and thrust his hand into Toshi's. Behind Marrow-Gnawer, the top of the yuki-onna's head rose, bringing her eyes level with the shelf.

Toshi quickly scratched a symbol into Marrow's hand and turned to Kiku. He held out his hand.

The jushi hesitated, took a last look at the snow woman, and gave Toshi her hand. He made the same mark, sheathed his jitte, and held on to Kiku's hand as he grabbed Marrow's.

"We are free," Toshi said, "bound only to each other. My life is yours, yours is mine. Harm one, harm all. The survivors must avenge. Whatever is taken from the hyozan, the hyozan recovers tenfold."

As he spoke, a cold wave passed through his hands to theirs. Kiku's spine stiffened, and she inhaled sharply. Marrow-Gnawer screeched in terror.

"She's here!"

Toshi held onto them. "Don't let go," he said. He stepped forward as the yuki-onna stretched out her hand. He kept his eyes fixed on her own terrible black wells.

The snow woman placed her hand on Toshi's forehead. He convulsed, almost crushing Kiku's hand and pulling Marrow's arm out of the socket. Ice formed in his eyebrows, and he felt his body temperature drop.

In the clearing, below the frozen corpses and a blanket of snow, the ring of symbols Toshi had made flashed to life. He had spent hours positioning the characters for his patron kami, his reckoner gang, and the cold embrace of endless shadow until they formed a ring on the ground. These symbols now glowed with an eerie purple light, the same light that now shone from Kiku's, Marrow's, and Toshi's linked hands.

The purple light flashed beneath the yuki-onna's palm where it touched Toshi. He heard a muffled explosion and felt a great concussion that drove him back. Kiku and Marrow-Gnawer came with him, and the snow woman herself was blown back like a leaf in a storm.

The dread spirit screeched as she plummeted to the ground. She landed within the ring of Toshi's glowing symbols, drawing the purple light from them to her like a lightning rod. Wailing, thrashing, the yuki-onna screamed so loudly that the stones around them cracked.

She was gone. The flickering lights vanished, the awful sound died away, and the three were left battered and dazed on the rocky shelf.

The terrible gloom dissipated, and the mid-morning sun returned. Toshi rose to his feet, peering down on the clearing. All of the snow that had fallen was gone, leaving the kanji and the corpses of Uramon's party behind.

Marrow-Gnawer was on all fours, praying and weeping. Kiku was on her haunches, leaning against the cliff face and rubbing the fresh mark on her hand.

"Welcome to the hyozan reckoners," he said.

"I'll kill you for this, Toshi."

"Not without consequences," he said cheerfully. He showed her his own hyozan tattoo on the back of his hand. "It would be extremely unlucky for any of us to turn on the others now. I'll give you a quick primer about how things operate in my gang. For now, let's just say that we're obliged to look after each other and enjoy the fact that we're all still alive, eh?"

Kiku snapped open her fan and sat heavily on the stone shelf. "Don't celebrate long, ochimusha. This is not over."

"In a way, it is."

"For now." Kiku primly adjusted her skirt. "What happens now?"

Toshi grinned mirthlessly. "We're already deep in the Sokenzan," he said. "I think a visit to your fellow reckoner and oath-brother would be in order."

Kiku snarled but held her tongue. "And after that?"

"After that, I think we should go back to Uramon. She's got something I want, so I'm going to offer her something she wants in exchange."

"What does she want?"

Toshi winked. "Me."

CHAPTER 6

Toshi led his new recruits east, toward the hinterlands that stood south of Towabara and west of the great Jukai Forest. Marrow-Gnawer was the first to realize the danger Toshi was steering them toward, as his keen sense of smell could scarcely miss the odor of fire and death growing ever closer. Kiku got wind of it, too, but she used her brain rather than her nose.

"You're taking us to the o-bakemono's home," she said. "His place of power." The jushi stopped where she stood. "I will go no farther."

"Hidetsugu calls his home Shinka," Toshi said lightly. "As he is one of the hyozan's founding members, he might take it as a slight if you didn't stop in to pay your respects."

On the path ahead, Marrow grumbled and moaned, his dark features twisted into a mask of anxiety.

Kiku shook her head. "There is bad blood between the ogre and my clan. Not to mention between him and Uramon."

"Plus, he'll eat us," Marrow added.

"There isn't enough meat on you to make a decent mouthful," Toshi replied. "Besides, he'd have to drain his well just to clean the stench of Takenuma off you." To Kiku, he said, "Don't be afraid, jushi. Even if I can't protect you, the hyozan oath will. I don't know why you can't accept that."

Kiku's temper flared. "The only things that frighten me are far beyond your meager comprehension, and as a rule, I refuse to accept anything that comes out of your mouth. An ogre shaman like him traffics with powerful oni, and those demons don't respect oaths."

"This one does," Toshi said seriously. "I've seen it in action, up close. It tore a big, blubbery fish kami to pieces like a pack of wild dogs, but it didn't even smack a lip in my direction. Hidetsugu will protect us."

"Hidetsugu is whom I wish to avoid."

Toshi shrugged. "Please yourself, but I learned a long time ago that it's better to have Hidetsugu on my side rather than elsewhere. I hope you live long enough to realize that."

Kiku's eyes narrowed, and the corner of her lips turned up in a cruel smile. "Is that a threat?" She opened her palm, displaying the hyozan mark. "'Oath-brother?'"

"It's a fact," Toshi said. "This place is thick with bandits and akki goblins. The akki might just kill you and use your bones as jewelry, but the sanzoku . . ." Toshi made a show of shivering. "I don't like to talk about what they might do."

Kiku tossed back her cloak, revealing the camellia on her shoulder and the wicked fuetsu throwing axe on her belt. "No one has laid hands on me and lived since I came of age."

Toshi snapped his fingers victoriously. "Then you've nothing to worry about. Meeting Hidetsugu should be nothing for a master jushi like yourself."

Kiku stared at Toshi for a moment, her expression growing ever darker. "Very well. I will accompany you, outlaw. It may be the only way to figure out how to break this hyozan bond you've shackled me with.

"But I shall not speak, and if your ogre so much as sniffs the air around me wrong, I will put this oath of yours to the test and plant flowers in all three of you." She turned to include Marrow-Gnawer in her threat, but the nezumi merely grumbled.

"Don't drag me in to your nightmare. I'm hoping he's extra hungry and eats you big jobbies first."

Toshi chuckled. "Hostility and cowardice. Just what I like to see in my reckoners."

"*Never* call me that." Kiku straightened her robe.

"Yeah," Marrow-Gnawer said. "When I left Numai, my pack was hunting you. If they find I've gone to work for you, they'll tear me apart."

They hiked on, silent but for Marrow's increasingly nervous sniffling. Soon they came to a deep, jagged valley with a wide dusty path leading down.

"Almost there," Toshi said. "Better let me go first. He's not the most hospitable person in the world."

At the edge of the descending path stood a row of tall wooden poles that stretched across the path like a fence. There were decapitated heads atop each pole, some human, some animal, and some of indeterminate origin. They were in varying stages of decay—some were freshly bleeding, most were buzzing with flies, and a few had been tanned and mummified by the cold, dry winds.

"See?" Toshi carefully stepped in between two poles, careful not to disturb them. He motioned for Kiku and Marrow to do the same.

As his two new partners navigated the ogre shaman's welcome

to passing strangers, Toshi carefully scanned each of the severed heads.

"Looking for a friend?" Kiku spat. She was brushing invisible bits of debris from her cloak, though she had been the most precise about avoiding the grisly trophies.

"Hardly," Toshi said, "but he's not here in any case." He did not elaborate, and Kiku did not press him.

Farther down the path, Kiku said, "The heads I understand. What is the significance of this pile of gravel?"

Toshi was staring at the mound of pebbles and broken rocks. The wind was steadily diminishing the pile, apparently as it had been for weeks. Toshi remembered the great rock that once stood here and calculated that more than half of its shattered substance was already gone. In a month or so, there would be no evidence that the huge square stone had ever blocked the path to Hidetsugu's hut.

"No idea," he said honestly. "Maybe our host will explain it to us." He waved his arm like a rich man presenting a banquet to his guests. "Let's keep moving, shall we? Shinka is just ahead."

From the surface, Hidetsugu's hut seemed like a small, one-room domicile. Toshi knew that it descended deep into the ground, expanding into a subterranean cavern that stretched for hundreds of yards beneath the valley floor.

Though he kept his feelings to himself, Toshi now felt an icy sense of dread in his stomach. When he had last left the o-bakemono, he had Hidetsugu's apprentice in tow. The ogre had described this student, Kobo, as exceptional. He had even insisted that Toshi add him to the ranks of the hyozan.

Toshi had not communicated with Hidetsugu since sending word of Kobo's death. Though he had sent the man responsible for the crime to face Hidetsugu's justice, Toshi was still reluctant to face his oath-brother. Kobo had died in his care, and ogres were famous for carrying grudges to irrational and violent extremes. Judging from the pile of gravel that used to be a gigantic boulder, Hidetsugu had taken Kobo's death very hard and was in turn taking it out on anything and everything around him. Indeed, reddish-black smoke now poured from the doorway to the ogre shaman's hut, fouling the air in the valley. The choking fumes burned Toshi's throat and drove Marrow-Gnawer to his knees, where he tried to suck clean air from ground level. Even Kiku had covered her mouth and nose with a square of purple silk.

"You look pale, outlaw." Kiku's voice was a study in vicious glee. "Having second thoughts?"

"Having trouble breathing," Toshi said. He cleared his throat and called out, "Hidetsugu. Oath-brother. Toshi Umezawa has returned, bearing news and allies."

Save for a thick stream of noxious smoke, no reply came from the hut. Toshi waited a few seconds then shrugged at Kiku and cupped his hand alongside his mouth.

"Hoy, ogre!" he yelled. "It's me, Toshi!"

The river of smoke ebbed, as if something huge were blocking the flow. Toshi heard a deep, full-throated growl that made his spine vibrate. Then a rough, raspy voice that was far more suited to roaring spoke in a gruff but quiet tone.

"Welcome, oath-brother."

Toshi could almost see a larger, denser shadow crouching among the darkness inside the hut's doorway.

"Come inside," Hidetsugu continued, his voice growing more distant and vague. "Bring your friends."

Toshi smiled unconvincingly at Kiku and Marrow. On the

whole, he would have preferred one of Hidetsugu's roared threats or even a demand to be let alone. He had business to discuss, however, hyozan business, and since the ogre shaman would never come to him . . .

"Let's go," Toshi said. Without waiting, he marched to the doorway and entered the hut.

The smoke and the smell were far worse inside. Toshi gagged, coughed, and struggled to take small sips of air through his mouth only. His eyes quickly adjusted to the interior of the dwelling, but if Hidetsugu had been here, he had also retreated into the recesses of his cavern.

Outside, Kiku was tying the silk kerchief over her face like a marauder's mask. Marrow-Gnawer plugged his nostrils with dirt. When the nezumi tried to enter the hut before the jushi, Kiku kicked him sharply in the ribs and pushed him down. She walked over his tail as she entered.

"You were right before," Toshi said. "Don't say anything to him unless you have to. Stay behind me and let me do the talking."

Kiku waved Toshi's concerns away, but she also took a half-step back and fell in behind him. Still grousing quietly to himself about the manners of supposedly cultured jushi, Marrow crept into the hut and waited behind Kiku.

Toshi led them down a steep incline, red smoke streaming across their faces and bodies. There was no way to avoid the stuff on the narrow ramp down. Toshi drew what breath he could and quickly descended into the cavern.

He stepped left at the bottom of the ramp and broke free of the smoke column. The air in the cavern was not sweet, but it was like a spring breeze compared to what he'd been breathing. He stood and waited as Kiku carefully lifted a corner of her mask, sniffed, then untied the kerchief. Marrow-Gnawer blocked one nostril with his finger, blew out the plug of dirt, and sniffed, clearing his nose completely.

Kiku scowled. "I am oath-bound to *that*?" she said, pointing at the nezumi. "I will absolutely kill you for this, Toshi."

"Wait until you see what else you're oath-bound to," Toshi observed. "Quiet, now. He's down here somewhere, but we won't find him until he wants us to."

The interior of the cavern was lit by a series of torches and braziers spaced randomly against the walls. Between the flickering shadows and the stark echoes it was impossible to gauge the size or shape of the space. Hidetsugu preferred it this way, though Toshi had never figured out if the ogre got around so easily because he knew the cavern's layout by heart or because he could see in the dark.

In any case, they were in the ogre's home and at his mercy. He would greet them—or not—at his leisure.

"Here," came the slow, ragged voice, calling from the far right of the cavern. "Come this way, my friends."

Kiku and Marrow-Gnawer did not move. Toshi took a tentative step forward. When nothing happened, he took another. Before he stepped outside of the dim circle of light cast by the nearby torch, he turned and gestured impatiently for Kiku and Marrow to follow.

"All three of you, yes." Hidetsugu's voice sounded as if he were smiling. "Just a little farther."

Feeling the ground before him with his toes extended, Toshi carefully picked his way across the stone floor. When his sandals touched the edge of a cavern wall, Toshi placed his hand on it and resumed walking normally, using the wall as a guide. He heard Kiku and Marrow-Gnawer do the same behind him. In near-perfect darkness, he led them along the wall and around a corner.

"That's far enough."

Toshi cleared his throat again. "Oath-brother," he said. "I need to talk to you."

"Talk."

"I'd prefer to see you. The smoke on the ramp has made me dizzy, and without light I fear I may swoon."

"Like a little girl," Kiku added. Marrow-Gnawer snickered.

"Quiet," Toshi hissed.

The ogre's growl silenced them all. "Very well," he said. Toshi heard the scrape of stone on stone behind Hidetsugu's voice. "I will give you fire as well as smoke."

There was a spark, and a flame flared above a burnished copper bowl. The brazier was wide but shallow, and as the fire rose from it the small chamber came into view. Hidetsugu was crouched over the brazier, his arms folded around his knees. There was room for him to stand, barely, but the massive ogre had curled himself into a tight knot of bulging muscles and tough, leathery hide. He was naked but for a black linen wrap that hung from his waist to his knees, and the visible portion of his torso was a mass of crisscrossing scars and burns.

The ogre shaman's head was broad and flat, wedge-shaped with a crest of bone running from his forehead to the back of his skull. Gnarled, slashing teeth jutted from his grinning lips, and his eyes reflected the firelight with a hellish red glow.

Pinned to the wall behind Hidetsugu were the headless corpses of four human beings, three male and one female. They were dressed in red and yellow breeches, and each wore either a circular medallion with a glyph inscribed across its center, or a tattoo of the same glyph across the breastbone. Their arms, legs, and hips were adorned with small red fetishes that reminded Toshi of the tassels on ceremonial swords.

Hidetsugu did not react as he let his eyes pass over Kiku and Marrow-Gnawer. Instead, he tilted his head back and opened his wide nostrils.

"You smell of Uramon," he told Toshi, "and something much more dangerous." The o-bakemono lowered his head and bowed.

"Welcome, fellow reckoners. I see Toshi has connived, cajoled, or convinced you to join our little enterprise." He shifted his weight and lowered one knee, revealing the hyozan mark branded into his shoulder. "He has a gift for persuasion."

Marrow-Gnawer silently bowed in return, lowering his eyes under the leather straps of his headdress. Kiku maintained her cool demeanor, but she kept glancing up at the bodies on the wall. Toshi saw shock in those cold black eyes.

"Yamabushi," Kiku hissed. "You've been collecting the kami-killers like butterflies."

Hidetsugu chuckled, a deep, rumbling laugh without joy. "I sought to enlist their aid. The first four elders refused. I had better luck recruiting their students. Would you like to meet them?"

"By all means," Toshi said. "After the introductions, though, we need to hold council. The hyozan still has work to do."

Hidetsugu shrugged. "Of course. First, come and meet my new apprentices."

They backed out of the alcove as the ogre lumbered forward, still crouching. Toshi was growing increasingly uncomfortable. Hidetsugu seemed lethargic, dazed, as if he'd been woken from a sound sleep, but a palpable air of menace came off him like a strong scent. Kiku and her fellow jushi regarded all o-bakemono as mad, and Toshi was inclined to agree, but this was the first time he'd seen Hidetsugu so listless, so disinterested. Toshi feared the inevitable storm that would follow this calm.

The ogre lit a torch from the wall and carried it with him straight across the center of the cavern. Toshi stayed as close as he dared, trying to keep within the small sphere of torchlight. Kiku and Marrow-Gnawer stayed well behind him, side-by-side, ready to bolt at the first sign of aggression.

The choking smell of smoke grew stronger than ever as they crossed the sea of darkness inside the cavern. Toshi could see hot ash and fumes overhead, and he reasoned they were approaching the source of whatever was producing the thick stream that flowed up the ramp.

"I imagine," Hidetsugu said casually, "that you've come about Kobo."

The ogre hadn't turned to address Toshi, and the ochimusha was grateful. He hesitated for a few paces, then said, "Yes, oath-brother. Among other things."

"Thank you, by the way, for sending that unexpected guest." Hidetsugu's voice sharpened, but he still maintained his maddening calm. He called back to the others, "You would do well to follow Toshi's example. He always honors his oath to his hyozan brothers."

"Is he—" Toshi began, but his words hitched in his burning throat. He started again, "Is the one who drowned Kobo outside?"

"On a pole? No, oath-brother. I extended my finest hospitality to him, made him feel as if he were at home. We've had pleasant dinner conversations for weeks now, and oh! the things he's told me."

Toshi gulped. He heard Kiku draw breath behind him, but before she could speak, Toshi said, "Don't ask."

Hidetsugu slotted the torch into a bracket on the cavern wall. They were outside another naturally occurring doorway, similar to the one in which they had found the ogre.

"Here we are," Hidetsugu said. He waved his massive arm toward the darkness and cocked his head. "After you."

Now at his full height, the ogre's lackadaisical attitude seemed far more paternal. Far more sinister. Toshi's well-developed sense of self-preservation was pounding in his ears like an extra pulse.

Toshi stepped into the darkened alcove. Kiku and Marrow-Gnawer came in behind him, as close as they could get without touching him.

He felt the ogre moving past him. Hidetsugu's footsteps faded as he crossed the alcove, and once more Toshi heard the sound of flint on stone. As another brazier flared to life, Hidetsugu said, "Oath-brothers, oath-sister. Behold the instruments of our reckoning."

Eight men and women kneeled in the flickering firelight, chained to one another at the neck with their hands and feet manacled. They were dressed in the red and white outfits of the yamabushi elders, but these mages were all physically intact. Some wore face paint, others wore carefully shaped beards, but all had black peaked phylacteries tied to their bald heads and long, flowing topknots hanging down past their shoulders.

Toshi had never seen such a collection of terrified faces. They were wide-eyed and slack jawed, and tear streaks cut through their war paint. Some had the vacant stare of combat veterans who have fought one battle too many, while others had the cold, glassy stares of trauma victims who would one day pass along their pain to someone new.

By Toshi's estimation, the oldest of Hidetsugu's captives was no more than thirty. The youngest was barely nineteen. They had been broken, humbled, abused into acquiescence. They were dead but still conscious. They were damned but fully aware that their worst sins still lay ahead.

The yamabushi did not react to the torch, the visitors, or even Hidetsugu himself. They simply kneeled, their eyes fixed on yet another body pinned to the wall.

Toshi stifled a gag reflex. Here was the source of the red charnel smoke. The mutilated form on the wall had a rough-hewn crystal embedded in its chest that glowed with a dull orange sheen. Its flesh was blackened and brittle, and heat radiated from it like an over-stoked oven. The toxic flow of red gas and black ash billowed up from the body's surface like the smoke from a charcoal-burner's mound. Both arms and both legs ended in stumps, roughly severed below the elbow and knee joints.

Toshi stared at the figure's head. Though its face had been almost completely obliterated by repeated blows and the intense heat from the gem, its hair remained intact. Toshi lowered his gaze from that close-cropped white-blond mane, unsure if he should admit that he now recognized the figure or if he should let Hidetsugu have the pleasure of revealing it.

The ogre was standing midway between the yamabushi and the figure on the wall. He was watching Toshi closely. The o-bakemono's voice was that of a genial host, but his words were steeped in malice.

"This is Choryu, a prodigy from Minamo Academy. He is also the agent of the academy elders and their soratami handlers. It was at their suggestion that he drowned Kobo while my most excellent apprentice was unconscious and bound. For this I have rewarded him with a taste of what awaits him in the afterlife, when my oni claims his soul." Hidetsugu turned to Toshi. "You did well in sending him to me, oath-brother. You will always have my thanks for that."

Toshi nodded, his expression as blank as those of the yamabushi.

"The hyozan demands satisfaction. Has Toshi taught you the words?"

Before Marrow-Gnawer or Kiku could answer, Toshi said, "I have not, but I will, in time."

Hidetsugu shrugged. "No matter. It's a lovely little verse about the extent of our vengeance, the scope of your suffering once you cross the hyozan. Suffice to say—" Hidetsugu's eyes flared, spitting fire into the brazier—"it's extensive."

A low, fearful sound rose up from the captive yamabushi.

Toshi stepped forward. "I won't deny your right to invoke our oath, but you'll forgive me if I notice that you've already got the man who did it." He gestured at the horror pinned to the wall. "I don't see how Kobo's reckoning could be more complete."

Hidetsugu's eyes grew dreamy. "Day and night," he said, "he burns without being consumed. He is cooked, but his flesh never falls from the bone. He blackens, but he does not crumble into ash.

"He starves. When he is on the point of passing, I feed him a snack from his own body. Day by day, inch by inch, he consumes himself. Toes and fingers first, then palms and soles. Eventually, he will taste his own vitals. What he consumes is not replenished, and still he does not die.

"His flesh is corrupt, suffuse with a poison that is far beyond the most toxic forest serpent. Each mouthful sears his insides, liquefies him from the inside out. His guts heave and twist, his stomach and bowels cramp and spasm to the point of bursting."

Hidetsugu fell onto his outstretched palms, his face mere inches from Toshi's, and the cavern walls shook.

"No, oath-brother, I am still not satisfied. The hyozan's reckoning is meant to be total, complete, to utterly crush any possibility of response. It is meant to punish every living thing connected to the transgressor, every institution with which he associates, even the very gods to whom he prays.

"I have gathered these mages because they are trained in the art of striking down kami. The hermits of Sokenzan long ago mastered the art of destroying spirits that journey from their world to this one. These—" he waved at the captives—"are their children, but they are also my instruments."

Toshi nodded slowly, holding Hidetsugu's ferocious gaze. "You want the hyozan to make war on the academy. To storm the waterfall, raze the soratami city in the clouds, and murder the kami that both wizard and soratami worship."

Hidetsugu rocked back and crossed his legs beneath him so that he and Toshi were still at eye-level.

"I do. First, though, I will pay a visit to the snakefolk and their human collaborators in Jukai Forest. The academy pup killed Kobo, but it was the worshipers of the forest myojin who made it possible. My apprentice could have swallowed a flood-swollen river and pissed it back in the wizard's face before it drowned him. The snakes laid him low and restrained him, made him vulnerable." Hidetsugu's diffuse vacancy was melting under the force of his fury. His eyes glowed a dull red. "The reckoning has only just begun, oath-brother."

Something creaked and crackled overhead. Toshi reflexively looked up, even as his better judgment screamed at him to shut his eyes.

On the wall, the ruined figure of Choryu the wizard stirred. Flakes of blackened skin drifted to the cavern floor. The yama-bushi keened again.

Two holes opened up in the swollen smear of a face. Choryu's eyes were gone. He opened his mouth. Air wheezed through his throat, producing a ghastly, gurgling, tongueless moan.

The yamabushi picked up the sounds of suffering and echoed it back against the stone walls. Among the chorus of wails and lamentations, Hidetsugu began to laugh.

Toshi turned to Kiku and Marrow-Gnawer. "Wait outside," he said quietly.

Kiku nodded, but Marrow shivered and wrapped his arms around his torso.

"Go on," Toshi said. "Get clear of the entrance and wait for me. You'll be safe."

"What about you?"

Toshi locked eyes with Kiku. "The founding members of the hyozan have to talk."

CHAPTER 7

Lady Pearl-Ear's captivity came to a sudden end. During breakfast she was still a prisoner, confined at the daimyo's behest. After her morning meal, the soldiers came into her cell, removed her manacles, and told her she must go.

She asked about an audience with the daimyo and the chance to bid Princess Michiko farewell, but the soldiers' orders were precise. Lady Pearl-Ear of the kitsune was to be released and escorted to the borders of the realm, forbidden to return. She was not to see or speak to anyone on the way.

It did not take Pearl-Ear long to prepare. She had no personal effects, and her cell was sparsely furnished. The guards offered her a small parcel tied up with string, but she did not open it to inspect the contents. They told her it was from her former classroom, where she had tutored Michiko in the history of Kamigawa and instructed her in the ways of diplomacy.

Bearing the small parcel under one arm, Pearl-Ear followed the sentries up to ground level and out through the tower gates. She saw bitter loss and confusion on the faces of humans she passed, but no one spoke or acknowledged her. Numb, weary, and concerned for the princess, Pearl-Ear walked in silence for the better part of a day until she and her escorts reached the border between the daimyo's kingdom and the Jukai Forest. Farther north lay kitsune territory and Sugi Hayashi, her own home village.

Pearl-Ear bowed to the guards as they turned to go. Only one returned her gesture—the rest were too bent on being shut of their charge who had so enraged the daimyo. She stood quietly with her hands folded around the parcel until the last soldier vanished from sight.

Pearl-Ear's reserve fell from her, and she darted into the cover of the nearby trees. With her fingers working the string around the parcel, she raised her head, oriented herself toward home, and began to run. It would take a human several days to reach her village, but a kitsune at full speed could do it in less than half that time. Her people were graceful and quick, and she knew this route well. She barely needed to watch where she was putting her feet as she navigated around exposed roots and low-hanging branches.

The last of the parcel's covering fell away. Still moving forward at a ferocious rate, Pearl-Ear peered down at the bundle between her gray-furred paws.

Her white teacher's robe had been freshly laundered, starched, and folded into a neat square with sharp corners. Pearl-Ear tossed it aside with barely a second glance.

Beneath the robe were two thick scrolls: a historical reference about the spiritual practices of her people, which Michiko-hime had requested and Pearl-Ear had sent up from her village. The second scroll was a collection of progress reports outlining Michiko's course of study, written in Pearl-Ear's own hand. She tucked these away inside her prisoner's garb without breaking the rhythm of her run.

The final item was a small piece of jewelry—an elegant gold cameo on a silver chain. Pearl-Ear thumbed the catch and opened the cameo, revealing an ink drawing of Lady Yoshino, the daimyo's favored concubine and mother of Michiko. The opposite face of the cameo carried a fine sketch of the princess herself.

Pearl-Ear clicked the cameo shut and looped the chain around her neck. She redoubled her efforts, running faster and faster until the trees themselves became a blur around her.

She could not leave Michiko under lock and key in the daimyo's tower. She would return to her people and consult the elders. Pearl-Ear could not free Michiko by force of arms, and she would not free her through stealth or trickery. With the Sugi Hayashi elders behind her, she could raise a delegation of kitsune diplomats and send them to petition Konda on his daughter's behalf. Pearl-Ear herself might be exiled, but she would drill the delegation in all the proper procedures and give them the arguments that would stir Konda to mercy. He *must* be made to see that Michiko was not only blameless but also in great danger without the full attention and support of her father.

The forest called out to her as she ran. The air was cleaner here, tinged with the scent of cedar, and it felt soothing on her face. The air in Eiganjo was stale and smelled of decay, even outside the walls of her cell. Sunlight streamed down through the cedar leaves and droplets of dew fell as birds lighted on branches.

Her people were a curious mix, wild and solitary on one hand, maintaining political and social intercourse with the humans of Towabara on the other. Though her thoughts were wholly given to Michiko's well-being, Pearl-Ear's heart sang at the opportunity to run free through the wild once more. Living in the tower had been bad enough; living under it in a window-less room had been even worse. Now that she was free, she could feel the life slowly flowing back into her. Until now, she had not realized how dead captivity had made her feel.

Exultant but ever-mindful of her duty, Pearl-Ear ran on.

* * * * *

Pearl-Ear reached Sugi Hayashi as the last rays of sun were withdrawing behind the horizon. Her legs had lost much of their muscle tone during her confinement, and though they pained her now she felt as if she could run for another day, another three days if she had to.

The sight of her village hit her like a blow in the stomach, however, crippling her forward momentum. She stumbled and staggered as she came to a halt, her eyes wide and her hands clenching.

Sugi Hayashi was no longer a village but a scattered pile of debris. Farmer's fences had been trampled, and the villagers' homes burned. The great square, where elders like Lady Silk-Eyes once addressed the population, had been broken like a dry field under the plowshare. Where dozens of kitsune had once kneeled and prayed, now there were only great clods of earth and jagged rocks. All around, smoke rose from the debris, filling the site of the former village with a pale gray fog that reminded Pearl-Ear of Eiganjo. Had the Kami War come here with the same force it had attacked the tower? Or was this the punishment handed down by an angry daimyo for what he saw as the kitsune betrayal of his trust?

Pearl-Ear stifled a sob. She clutched the cameo around her neck and went into the village, shuffling like a sleepwalker. Ahead was the dwelling in which Elder Silk-Eyes lived, now an obscene tangle of broken wood and burned soil. Farther on were the barracks where Captain Silver-Foot and his retainers stayed between patrols through the woods. Over to her left was the home she and her family had lived in as kits, the same one she had visited briefly before Michiko left the tower.

The reason for the village's destruction came to her, and she was ashamed not to have recalled it sooner. What drove her and Michiko from the village so many weeks before, one of the many reasons she could not have returned the princess to Konda before she did, was the same thing that had leveled Sugi Hayashi.

At the time, an unusual force of sanzoku bandits and mountain akki had been moving through the forest. Pearl-Ear's village was in their path. After conferring with the political and military authorities responsible for the village, they all agreed to take Michiko-hime away to safety while Captain Silver-Foot and a contingent of the daimyo's cavalry held the raiders off. Pearl-Ear and a hand-picked team of escorts had led the princess away from this battle but into a far more dangerous encounter.

Pearl-Ear tore her thoughts back to the present. She had escaped with Michiko before the marauding horde reached the village and had been pursued, pursuing, or imprisoned ever since. She had no idea what happened here.

Concentrating, opening her senses, Pearl-Ear tried to determine the course of events. There were no traces of the villagers, but that did not surprise her—kitsune were expert at not being discovered. There was precious little evidence that the enemy had been here, either, apart from the occasional flash of akki rage and sanzoku brutality. If the raiders had prevailed, why weren't there more signs of them? If the villagers had won, who had destroyed the village?

"Dreadful, isn't it?"

Pearl-Ear started, clutching at her cameo as she spun to face the source of the sound. There, on the edge of the tree line, leaned a small male kitsune. He was lithe and compact, with a mischievous gleam in his eye.

"Hello, sister," the newcomer said. "I respected what I'm sure were your wishes and left you in the daimyo's prison. As you have noticed—" he spread his arms wide—"there have been some changes while you were away."

"Sharp-Ear, my brother," she said. "You were right to wait. I am back now, and I am glad to see you."

"And I you." Sharp-Ear bowed gracefully, then slouched back against the tree. "Konda sent word that you were being released . . . or rather, one of his generals did."

"That would have been General Takeno," Pearl-Ear said. "He was always a man of honor."

Sharp-Ear nodded. "He also said that Konda was through with our village and that he never wanted to see another kitsune in Eiganjo again." The little fox-man waggled his eyebrows. "I take it the daimyo was not so overjoyed by the return of his daughter that he forgot who was minding her when she left?"

"That is an understatement. I was treated like a criminal, shackled, isolated, forbidden even to go outside. Michiko as well. I'm sure it's much worse for her, poor girl."

Sharp-Ear's playful expression did not change, but Pearl-Ear heard anger under her brother's playful façade. "And the ochimusha who compounded my error and abducted the princess? What of Toshi Umezawa?"

"Still at large, as far as I know, but I'm not in much of a position to comment on current events."

"Indeed. Would you care for a quick lesson?"

"I would, brother. I am full of questions. How did the battle go? Where is Silk-Ear? Where is Silver-Foot? Where are the rest of the villagers?" She spread her arms out, mimicking Sharp-Ear's earlier gesture. "Where is the village?"

Sharp-Ear cocked his head, amused. He beckoned Pearl-Ear toward him. "Walk with me," he said, as he turned and strode into the forest. "By the time I answer the first question, you will see the answers to the rest."

* * * * *

Sharp-Ear had always been a storyteller, and he warmed to his subject as he and Pearl-Ear made their way through the trees.

"As you recall," he said, "the daimyo's cavalry charged the akki before they ever reached the village. I was with them for that. If there had been but two hundred, or even three, we would have slaughtered the lot of them before they ever set foot in Sugi Hayashi. However, there were more than we expected, more than there could have been. We always knew akki bred quickly, but their patron kami must have blessed them. Their numbers seemed to double every few days."

Pearl-Ear scowled at the thought of an extended siege. "How long did the final battle last?"

"Only a few hours. Silver-Foot and his retainers more than made up for the debacle in the forest. I'm told that less than a score of kitsune managed to hold off the entire horde for an hour without taking a single casualty of their own." Sharp-Ear scowled but shook off his troubling thoughts. "It made all the difference to be defending instead of attacking. They forced the advancing akki into a single choke point, rendering their superior numbers meaningless. Blade-Tail told me the blood was so thick that akki corpses actually floated away.

"Then, a gift from the spirits: Captain Nagao, commander of the daimyo's forces here, was brought in alive from the massacre in the woods."

"You said he was dead."

"I was sure of it. He took an arrow to the chest and a long fall from his horse. I dragged him as far as I could with my broken arm, but in the end I had to leave him to get back here and warn the village. Perhaps if I had been stronger, he could have saved even more of his riders from the akki."

Pearl-Ear hiked on in silence for a few paces. "You are remarkably contrite, brother." It was true—her brother usually never brooded about his follies. Most times, in fact, he seemed to take perverse pleasure in admitting his best intentions when his half-baked schemes had gone awry.

"I have grown in the past few months, sister. Not matured, mind you, for that is still beyond the scope of possibility, but even I cannot avoid the truth. I made a series of poor decisions, ones that have brought much grief to those I love and respect. Nagao could call me a coward, and I would not be able to rebut him."

"I can, brother, and I will. You are no coward, Sharp-Ear."

"Thank you. I will endeavor to deserve that high opinion. Now, back to my tale. While the kitsune samurai battled the akki to a standstill, our rangers worked their way around the horde on each side. We knew they were being led by twin sanzoku brothers . . . well, they were being led by one twin after I put an arrow through the other one's neck in the woods . . . but the plan was to capture, kill, or incapacitate the humans. Akki are not known for their brilliant battle tactics, you see. They tend to throw themselves at the enemy until one side or the other runs out of army. In this case, Silver-Ear and his men could have defeated a thousand akki who were following that plan.

"Alas, rapid reproduction was not the only blessing the raiders' myojin had bestowed. A minor kami was with them, a two-legged, goat-faced brute who belched out red-hot rocks like an erupting volcano. By the time our rangers realized that the humans had moved on, this kami had arrived on the front."

"The sanzoku left the goblins alone?"

"Yes. Whatever they were doing here in Jukai, they were confident enough to leave three hundred members of their horde behind just to flatten our village. The volcano kami was like an entire battery of heavy cannon, only far more mobile. We weren't prepared for that kind of fight.

"His first blast wiped out three akki for every one kitsune. Silver-Foot lost part of an ear and hasn't heard out of it since. And do you know what the akki did, when their own ally fired on them? Do you know what they said when burned bits of their friends and relatives fell on them like snow? They cheered. They howled and capered like the battle was already won.

"Oh, yes, they ran for their lives and cleared the field so they themselves wouldn't get blasted, but they celebrated their own destruction because it was a preview of ours.

"The volcano kami fired again, and again. Each time it launched a missile, kitsune fell, houses collapsed, fields went up in flames. We . . . they pierced him with a hundred arrows, but he still kept coming. He blew holes in our tight formations; he brought whole trees down in front of our advancing warriors. I believe he would have destroyed everything and everyone if given the chance. Fortunately, Lady Silk-Eyes had already led most of the villagers into the woods. She knew how to hide large groups. The akki could search for a year and they'd never find a single hair from her tail."

"This is terrible, Sharp-Ear. How did any of the warriors survive?"

"By stopping the kami in his tracks."

"But how?"

"It was Nagao's idea. He sent a message to Silver-Foot: the best way to stop a cannon is to cap it. He also sent four of his best riders on four of his biggest mounts. They lashed ropes to a section of tree trunk and slung it between them, two to a side. Then, they galloped straight at the kami and slammed the tree into him like it was a battering ram and his chest was the door."

Sharp-Ear turned and grinned. "Blade-Tail told me the kami fired right as the tree made contact. His shots were powerful, but the mass and momentum of the century cedar were more so. The explosion shattered half of the battering ram and killed two of the horses, but most of its fury was reflected back on the kami itself. When the smoke cleared, he was in three large pieces, still struggling. Silver-Foot himself put his sword through the kami's brain."

Pearl-Ear nodded. "What about the akki?"

"The rangers drove most of them back into the forest. The samurai mopped up those who remained. The villagers endured, but the village was lost. Elder Silk-Eyes says we will rebuild it, in time. For now, the kitsune of Sugi Hayashi are living as our ancestors did, wild and out of doors."

"I must speak with Silk-Eyes," Pearl-Ear said. "She and the other elders must authorize an official visit to Eiganjo on behalf—"

"Slow down, sister. We are almost there. Once we are, you can tell Silk-Eyes and the rest of us yourself."

For a moment, Sharp-Ear was again like his old self, playfully harboring a secret just for the sake of revealing it later. As touched as she was by his words of regret earlier, Pearl-Ear was heartened by the return of the energetic and conniving Sharp-Ear who exasperated her so often.

Like the village itself, her people had been bested but not beaten. As long as there were kitsune elders to offer wise counsel, kitsune warriors to fight, and kitsune tricksters to stack the deck in their favor, her people would endure.

If there was hope for them, perhaps there was hope for all Kamigawa.

CHAPTER 8

Toshi refused to talk in front of the yamabushi captives, so Hidetsugu led him to the far side of the darkened cavern. They entered yet another alcove, and Hidetsugu lit another torch.

The ochimusha let his eyes readjust to the low light and said, "What are you doing, oath-brother?"

Hidetsugu tilted his head. "You have answered your own question. I am living up to my oath with respect to Kobo. I expect no less from you."

"The man who killed Kobo is currently hanging from your wall."

"Indeed, but his is merely the hand that did the deed. I want the head that gave the order."

"So you murder four of the most dangerous mages in the Sokenzan, further antagonize their tribe by kidnapping their best students, and then brutalize them until they're conditioned as attack dogs for your kami hunt? This is not smart, Hidetsugu. This is not subtle. This is not good for business."

The ogre's eyes glowed like embers. "Our bond may be a formality of 'business' for you, ochimusha, but it is far more to me. I have dedicated my life to exploring the mysteries and the power of the oni. It is my chosen destiny. Kobo was to play a great role in that destiny."

Toshi paused. "Why did the wizard drown him?"

Hidetsugu only grinned. "Now Kobo is gone, but my destiny remains. I will do as I have always intended to do, Toshi Umezawa. In that, we are alike."

Toshi grimaced in frustration. "Listen to me. There's a lot more going on here than you know about. For once I have a clearer understanding of things than you do. You have to trust me, and follow my lead. Your way won't work."

Hidetsugu laughed. "Are you telling me you have a better one? That you are still pursuing Kobo's reckoning?"

"Of course not, but I could be. I can help you do this in a way that won't destroy us all."

"That's the difference between us, human. I embrace the inevitable while you seek to run from it." He leaned forward, his foul carrion breath stinging Toshi's eyes. "There is *no way* to avoid destroying us all. Life in the utsushiyo is brutal and short for pauper, daimyo, and o-bakemono alike—now more than ever, with things unraveling as they are. Chaos is coming to consume us all, Toshi. I welcome it. In fact, I will hasten its arrival.

The ogre's voice had dropped to a low growl. "I will have my reckoning and serve my oni, both at once. This is my choice."

"And I'm telling you to reconsider your choice." Toshi swallowed. Hidetsugu was intimidating, but he was still wrong. "You will get what you want, I swear it. Let me get what I want, as well. That is how the hyozan operates: we look out for each other's interests."

The o-bakemono snorted. "Now we get to the truth. What is it you want, Toshi? And how do you intend to use me to get it?

Perhaps it has something to do with the reek of kami magic that rises from you like cheap perfume."

Toshi's eyes narrowed. "Indeed it does. Is that a problem?"

"It could be. I preferred you as you were: incredulous of anything you couldn't control. If you've accepted some higher spirit as your patron, you're just another human bleating for salvation from the kakuriyo." Hidetsugu barked out another rough chuckle. "It will never come. The oni will claim us all in this world, and we will never see another."

Toshi hesitated. "That's not true, oath-brother. I have seen the other world."

The ogre's face lit up. "Aha! Then you have learned something crucial?"

"Perhaps. Have you learned anything crucial from what's left of the wizard?"

Hidetsugu displayed his horrible teeth. "Perhaps."

Toshi pulled back his sleeve and rotated his arm to display the hyozan tattoo emblazoned on the back of his hand. "An exchange of information, then. Let's hear each other out then we'll argue about whose course is the wisest."

Hidetsugu twisted at the waist to display his own hyozan mark. "I agree," he said. "You go first."

"I know what started the Kami War," Toshi said instantly. "The daimyo cast a spell. He reached into the spirit world and plucked something out. The kami are hostile because they want it back."

Hidetsugu placed a finger just under his lower lip. He concentrated, and Toshi almost laughed at the sight of a terrible creature striking such a studious pose.

"I believe you. What is the nature of the thing he stole?"

Toshi shook his head. "Your turn."

The ogre nodded, his gaze growing vacant. Suddenly he became alert, as if remembering Toshi was there. "The wizard says he murdered Kobo to please his soratami masters and their patron kami. Also, to protect the runaway princess. You didn't mention that you'd met the daimyo's daughter, Toshi." The ogre waggled his finger accusingly.

"I was getting to that," Toshi said. "How would removing us please the moonfolk?"

"The soratami are up to something grand. They are simultaneously infiltrating the Takenuma underworld and preparing for all-out war with the wild tribes of the Jukai Forest. Their kami wants them to avoid attracting attention until both offensives are in place.

"You, Toshi, stumbled across them in the ruins. Kobo was dressed in his tribal Jukai costume. The wizard panicked once the snakes captured everyone and decided to silence you both." The ogre smiled unpleasantly. "Also, I think he just didn't like you."

"I get that fairly often. You know, our new brother Marrow-Gnawer out there might be able to give us more information. He's already been recruited by the soratami. Uramon was going to force him to lead us to them."

"It's not a bad idea," Hidetsugu muttered. "Now it's your turn to share."

Toshi nodded. "The nature of the thing, yes. Princess Michiko was born on the night her father cast the spell. She's being kept under house arrest because she's somehow connected to the thing he stole from the kakuriyo. It's a powerful kami in the shape of a stone disk. The markings on its face display what looks like a fetal dragon."

For the first time since he'd met the ogre, Toshi saw shock on Hidetsugu's face. It was a brief flicker of raw emotion . . . not quite fear, but neither simply surprise.

Then the emotion was gone, and the shaman resumed his thoughtful pose. "A fetal serpent, perhaps?"

"Could be. There's a fine line between dragons and serpents, and the statue was rough-hewn."

"How did you come by this information?"

"Ah. It's your turn. Who is the kami behind all this? Who's guiding the moonfolk?"

Hidetsugu stared at Toshi, his finger over his chin. "I predict your question and mine have the same answer."

"What?"

"The soratami are guided by an aspect of the moon. Moon folk, moon kami. The wizard does not pray to him directly, but he knows its name. It is called the Smiling Kami of the Crescent Moon."

Toshi's belly went cold. He tried to gather his thoughts before Hidetsugu noticed his agitation.

But the ogre was too sharp. He seemed to be ready for Toshi's reaction. "Is this spirit familiar to you?"

Toshi nodded. "He introduced himself," he said. "Little blue fellow, on the chubby side. He told me to call him Mochi."

* * * * *

Lady Pearl-Ear's hopes were raised even farther when the makeshift village came into view. The refugees from Sugi Hayashi had taken to the wild without any apparent interruption in their tranquil lifestyle. As Pearl-Ear and Sharp-Ear approached, she saw kitsune craftsmen constructing shelters, herders driving their flocks, and even a small group of kits playing a chasing game through the massive cedars. Their robes were threadbare and their bodies lean, but the foxfolk seemed more comfortable and at peace than ever.

"She's back," called a voice from the top of a nearby tree. "Lady Pearl-Ear has returned!"

Pearl-Ear watched as the agile kitsune sentry leaped down, half-running and half-falling to the ground. He landed in a graceful roll and came up into a bow on the path in front of Pearl-Ear and her brother.

"Welcome, Pearl-Ear." Dawn-Tail was one of the kitsune warriors who had accompanied Pearl-Ear on her mission to rescue the princess. He and his brothers had been instrumental in keeping the group alive and together throughout the difficult journey.

"Thank you, Dawn-Tail. Are your noble brothers Blade-Tail and Frost-Tail well?"

"They are waiting for you, Lady. As are the elders. Please follow me."

They fell in behind the nimble warrior as he trotted into the collection of huts and lean-tos. Pearl-Ear craned her head to whisper at Sharp-Ear. "Elders? Our village has only ever had one."

"And one is all we have, but we are not the only village represented at this historic gathering."

"Historic? Sharp-Ear, what are you talking about?"

"Shh. We're almost there."

"I insist—"

Pearl-Ear's words died unuttered as she entered the large,

circular clearing. She could almost hear Sharp-Ear beaming beside her.

Dawn-Tail trotted into the assembly and took his place at the front, alongside his brothers. Frost-Tail and Blade-Tail both tipped their heads to Pearl-Ear then resumed standing at attention.

There were over fifty kitsune samurai and rangers assembled into one great company. Behind them in a smaller unit were a dozen or more human soldiers. They were all dressed in gleaming white robes and pieces of polished leather armor. Their swords glinted in the sun that filtered through the cedar canopy.

Captain Silver-Foot of the kitsune and Captain Nagao of Towabara both stood on a broad tree stump overlooking the soldiers. Silver-Foot nodded to Pearl-Ear, and Nagao shouted a single command. The soldiers all stood at ease.

On another stump opposite Silver-Foot stood five white-robed kitsune elders. They were bent and wizened, the fur around their muzzles flecked with white. Pearl-Ear recognized Lady Silk-Eyes, the elder from her own village, but the others were strangers to her. She had been an ambassador among humans for so long that she was a stranger to the tribal politics of her own people.

"Hail, Lady Pearl-Ear," Silk-Eyes said. The elder might have seemed withered by age, but she was smarter and craftier than any ten of her villagers and nearly as nimble. "Welcome home."

Pearl-Ear blinked tears from her eyes as she approached the stump-dais. She bowed. "Thank you, elder. Though home is not as I recall it."

"It never is, my child. As pleased as we are to see you again, you must know that all this is not simply for you."

"I should hope not, elder."

Silk-Eyes indicated the other elders. "We petitioned the daimyo on your behalf. I believe he would have released you eventually of his own accord, but I flatter myself that our request helped him decide."

"Of course. You have my thanks, elders, all of you."

"Understand that we have severed most ties with Konda. This was not done in response to your imprisonment, nor was it done with rancor. We believe that the daimyo can no longer protect us from our common enemies. He agreed to let us protect ourselves as we see fit.

"Privately, I believe he was happy not to have the extra drain on his resources. The Kami War has always been centered on Konda's domain. True, it has spilled out of his nation and spread across the land until nowhere is safe, but the tower at Eiganjo is the least safe of all. I pray for those who have taken refuge there—it will be a long time yet before their tribulations end."

A solemn murmur of assent swept through the assembly. Pearl-Ear and many others bowed her heads.

Silk-Eyes continued. "Your trials are far from over too, Lady Pearl-Ear. We have been awaiting your return, but not idly. We are sending an official delegation on behalf of all the great tribes and villages. If you are willing, we would have you sit at the head of that delegation to plead our case."

Pearl-Ear stood up straight. "I am forbidden to return to Konda's realm, elder, but I will not—"

Sharp-Ear elbowed her as Silk-Eyes smiled patiently.

"We do not wish to send you back to the daimyo in Eiganjo. We wish you to petition the wizards of Minamo academy for their counsel during this crisis."

Pearl-Ear was stunned. "I don't understand," she said.

"You don't need to understand," Sharp-Ear whispered. "Just say yes."

"But I—"

Silk-Eyes turned and called, "Bring her out." She faced Pearl-Ear once more and said, "Shortly after you were imprisoned, we received a guest from the academy. She sought my advice. Ah, here she is now."

A thin figure in pale blue and white robes climbed up onto the stump. She bowed to the elders, then stood beside Silk-Eyes. The newcomer lifted her hands and peeled her hood back from her face.

"Lady Pearl-Ear," said Riko-ome. "It is good to see you again."

"Riko?" Pearl-Ear was amazed to see the princess's closest friend here in the wilds of Jukai. Riko was a top student at the academy and a frequent guest of Michiko's at the tower. The two were closer than sisters, and Riko had accompanied Michiko on the princess's ill-advised flight from the tower.

"I am pleased to see you, Riko, but what are you doing here?"

Riko's lip trembled as she glanced to the elder. "I . . . learned something when I returned to Minamo. Something important that could help Michiko. But I was prevented from learning enough to actually do anything.

"I have no sway with the masters at the academy. I'm just a student. If the kitsune were to ask my questions, though, even the headmaster himself would be loath to refuse."

Pearl-Ear nodded, but her voice was full of concern. "I think I understand, Riko, but are you really prepared to plot against your own mentors? Helping us against them will seem very much like a betrayal. Perhaps it is. Are you ready for the consequences?"

Riko straightened her back and tossed her short brown hair away from her face. "I am. For Michiko, I am."

"We are all prepared to make sacrifices," Silk-Eyes said. She gestured at Captain Nagao, who offered a stiff half-bow, the wound in his chest preventing anything more. "Some of us have already given too much and yet are willing to give more. This is the position I must place you in, Pearl-Ear. Sharp-Ear is clever, but he is not well schooled in dealing with humans. Our delegation has a much greater chance of success if you are leading it."

Pearl-Ear glanced around at the assembly. Her heart swelled as her eyes passed over the proud and eager faces of the warriors and the grim but resolute expressions on Silver-Foot and Nagao. The elders all smiled patiently, but Riko's face was open, pleading. Pearl-Ear turned to Sharp-Ear.

He winked. "Come on, sister. Let's stop this while we can."

Pearl-Ear exhaled. She turned back and bowed to Silk-Eyes and the other kitsune elders.

"I am at your service," she said. "When do we go?"

Silk-Eyes beamed. "Now," she said. "Right now."

* * * * *

Hidetsugu laughed aloud at the name. "Mochi?"

"That's what he said. He looked like a bloated little kappa without its shell, but he was powerful—he proved that. I figured he was playing me for a fool somehow, but I didn't imagine . . ." Toshi's voice trailed off as his thoughts raced.

Hidetsugu crouched down and settled against the cavern wall. "Moon spirits are all tricksters. The soratami believe themselves descended from a moon myojin. They say that's why they're so mysterious and clever, and why they look down on the rest of us."

"It doesn't fit," Toshi said. "He was trying to get the princess to safety. There was a soratami present when Konda cast his spell, and a Minamo wizard, I saw it. But Mochi told Michiko not to go near the academy . . ."

"This all just proves my case," Hidetsugu said. "Even if you figure out what this Mochi's angle is, would it matter? His motives are unimportant. What matters is that he caused Kobo's death, so he and his soratami followers will die."

Toshi looked up at the ogre. He chose his words very carefully.

"I agree. But I think there is a way where we can both be satisfied and still conclude the hyozan's business. I just need some time."

Hidetsugu glared suspiciously. "How much time?"

"A few days. Maybe a week. How long will it take you to reach the academy?"

The ogre snarled savagely. "Not long."

"Then you must wait a week or so before you go."

"Must I? Tell me why."

"Because I need to collect one last item. I'm sort of on a pilgrimage, what with my newfound religion and all."

Hidetsugu grunted. "That's *why* you want me to wait, not why I *should*."

Toshi felt he was losing the argument or at least losing Hidetsugu's interest. He needed to do something drastic to regain the ogre's attention.

"Your oni," Toshi said. "It's the Big Bad Oni of Chaos, right?"

Hidetsugu's nostrils flared. "Respect, oath-brother. He is called the All-Consuming Oni of Chaos."

"Chaos," Toshi echoed. "What if I gave you the means to spread chaos? To drop a huge lump of it into the daimyo's lap?"

"If you could do that, I would want to hear more. Can you do that?"

Toshi reached into his pack. "I can," he said. "With this."

He drew out a plate-shaped object and held it out to Hidetsugu. It looked and felt like polished black stone, with a deep blue vein running across its face. The vein formed a kanji that glittered in the torchlight.

Hidetsugu stared for a moment. "You," he said at last, "are truly mad, Toshi Umezawa."

"I get that a lot, too." He waggled the inscribed plate. "What's your decision? All you need to do is take this to any one of a dozen spots along the border where the bandits and the daimyo's troops are testing each other. Break the seal, and stand back."

Hidetsugu never took his eyes off the object in Toshi's hand. "If I agree, that still leaves me the better part of a week to sit and wait. I cannot rely on my patience, Toshi, and neither can you."

"Never crossed my mind." Toshi lowered the plate, flexing his arm to get the blood flowing again. The temperature in the alcove had begun to drop, and his fingers were tingling.

"You said you had a score to settle with the Jukai Myojin as well. When you've placed this seal, gather your yamabushi and head into the forest. Amuse yourself among the *orochibito* snakefolk and tear a few pieces out of their kami. If it's the one with the wooden mask of a woman's face, tell her Toshi sends his regards."

Toshi did a quick calculation in his head. "Stay away from the academy until the moon begins to wax. It's waning now and will be completely dark in few days. A few days after that, it'll start to come back. Give me that much time at least. I'll meet you on the edge of the waterfall and we can avenge Kobo together."

Toshi drew close to the ogre and lowered his voice, putting forth all the intensity at his command. "Do it," he urged. "Do it because it's good business. Do it because it means a more complete reckoning. Do it so I won't have to point out that Kobo may have died on my watch, but it was you who insisted on sending him with me. We barely made it into the forest before we were jumped by a bunch of akki and bandits who were summoning their patron kami. Were you trying to test Kobo against their myojin, or was it just a happy coincidence?"

Hidetsugu's hand flashed out and clamped around Toshi's chest. The ogre lifted him to his face, his eyes wild.

"What I did was a mistake," he growled, "but not the mistake that killed him. Nor was it as grave an error as what you just said to me."

"I am your oath-brother," Toshi countered. "You won't hurt me. Put me down."

Hidetsugu held him firmly, but he was not crushing Toshi. The ochimusha could breathe freely.

The ogre dropped Toshi to the cavern floor as suddenly as he'd scooped him up. "If I take this thing—" he gestured to the plate in Toshi's pack—"then you must accept something from me. A token similar to yours."

Toshi climbed back to his feet. "I'll take all the help I can get.

The quicker I finish, the quicker we get to the academy."

Hidetsugu stood and lumbered off into the dark recesses of the cavern. When he returned, he carried something in his clenched fist. The ogre sat once more against the wall and extended his hand to Toshi.

Toshi cupped his palms, and Hidetsugu opened his fist. A single red mosaic tile dropped into Toshi's hands.

He peered in the dim light. "I can't read it."

Hidetsugu grunted and clapped his hands. All around the alcove, torches sprang to light.

Toshi looked around, the tile in his hands all but forgotten. The alcove was covered from floor to ceiling in a series of black and red tiles depicting an endless sea of razor-toothed mouths. They were disembodied, slavering, countless as they covered the walls like a swarm of bees. At the center of the longest wall, three huge and baleful eyes glared down, flanked on each side by a curved horn.

The All-Consuming Oni of Chaos. Toshi had seen altars to this demonic presence in Hidetsugu's home, but there was no altar here, just the overwhelming sensation of being surrounded and doomed at the center of this storm of voracious jaws.

"Well?" Hidetsugu said. "Can you read it now?"

Toshi glanced down. The red tile was inscribed with an elegant line drawing of a monstrous dog. It was armored and massive in the chest, thin and wasted at the rear. It had the characteristic three eyes and twin curved horns of an oni.

"I've seen this before," Toshi said. "This monster. Kobo summoned it to fight the akki myojin and its lesser kami."

"It is a minor oni, one of the dogs of bloodlust. Crack the tile when you need its help. Be sure you are the first thing it sees, for it will kill everything else in its range until the summoning charm wears off."

"How wide is its range?"

"Farther than any man can run," Hidetsugu said, "and it is much faster."

"I will accept your gift," Toshi said, "if you will accept mine." He indicated the plate-sized seal in his hand. "And if you will wait until the new moon waxes."

He held the seal out. Hidetsugu sat nodding for a moment then said, "Done." He extended his upturned palm.

Toshi dropped the cold black disk and tucked the red tile into his pack. "So we are agreed."

The ogre shaman nodded. "We are, but the countdown has begun. I advise you to conclude your business as quickly as you can, for there will be no academy to visit once I arrive."

Toshi glanced up at the walls and the omnipresent specter of Hidetsugu's oni. He pictured the dead-eyed yamabushi elsewhere in the cavern. He looked up at Hidetsugu, a crouching mass of muscle and rage-fueled cruelty.

He said a silent prayer to his myojin, not on his behalf or even for the academy's but for a more simple gift. All over the world, it seemed time was running out.

CHAPTER 9

The sanzoku bandit king rode up the ridge overlooking the border between Towabara and the Sokenzan Mountains. Godo was a huge man, broad and powerful, but he seemed even larger and more formidable mounted atop his burly mountain yak. His huge bald head steamed in the cold, and his thin top-knot twisted in the breeze behind him. Three long spears sprouted from the back of his saddle, and a huge, spiked log on a chain thudded against the yak's thick fur.

Some said that Godo didn't fight with the log but instead hurled it to his enemies as a weapon for them to use. Those that weren't crushed by it exhausted themselves trying to lift it. The truth was, Godo could swing the heavy log like a stone in a sling with enough force to kill both horse and rider in one blow.

He was more than forty years old and had been leading raids on the daimyo's kingdom for over half his life. He was a member of the oldest mountain tribe, and his parents and grandparents had fought to keep Konda from turning the Sokenzan into another subjugated province. Let the foxes wax philosophic about living under a tyrant and the wizards rush to serve their new king. The people of the mountains were wild and rough, but they understood freedom.

The mountains were still technically free, but they were isolated from the rest of Kamigawa's tribes by distance as well as the daimyo's edicts and the soldiers he stationed to keep the mountain tribes contained. Let them keep their wasteland, Konda was rumored to have said, for it is all they will ever have.

Godo always smiled when he thought of Konda's words. The daimyo's army was superior to all of the bandit warriors combined—better trained, better equipped, and better fed. But even they had not been able to make Konda's dire proclamation come true. Godo and his sanzoku had thrived for more than a decade on whatever they could raid from Konda's territory. The daimyo's subjects paid taxes for the privilege of eking out an existence on the borderlands; Godo and his followers simply rode in and took it.

Their routes in and out of Towabara changed with the seasons, but Godo always managed to find a way. In the past few years, as the Kami War had escalated out of control, Konda's diligence on the border had suffered. He simply didn't have the numbers to cover the entire border, and his farmers couldn't produce enough food to feed them if he did.

Godo had spent the past few days riding the ridge, looking for the next winter route that would allow his men to slip inside Konda's borders. There were almost no settlers left within easy reach, no working farms within striking distance. Their raids had to go ever deeper into Konda's territory in order to find anything worth taking. Godo's troops were in for a rough few months unless they could find enough stores to last until spring or else establish a reliable route in and out of Towabara.

Now that he had reached an accord with the akki who lived in this region, he was free to scout locations his raiders could use as temporary bases. Weeks ago, he had sent his two best lieutenants—the Brothers Yamazaki, Seitaro and Shujiro—on a special mission deep into Konda's territory. The plan had come to Godo in a dream, perhaps in response to his people's prayers.

The Myojin of Infinite Rage told him to send raiders to the heart of Eiganjo, where the daimyo's tower stood. A successful raid on the tower would yield enough plunder to keep half of their tribe alive for the winter. It would also force Konda to direct more of his troops away from the border. Konda's people would continue to suffer, which meant Konda himself would also suffer.

Over the years, Godo's hatred for Konda's regime had become a constant, grinding ache. Despising Konda, harming Konda had become Godo's religion, and his myojin was quick and generous with its blessings.

Godo slowed the great yak and listened intently. The Sokenzan Range was a dangerous place, even for bandits. There were powerful entities to be consulted or appeased before he could lead his troops safely through this patch of rocky ground. The akki nation was the least of them, but even they were too troublesome to simply dismiss. And it was always treacherous negotiating passage through o-bakemono country. At least this time the ogre had offered to come to him.

Satisfied he was not being followed, Godo prodded the yak. Together they crested the ridge, where Godo caught sight of the o-bakemono. It was rare to see Hidetsugu outside of his valley, but the shaman had gone wild lately, venturing into the Jukai on his own private raids. The day before, he had contacted Godo with an offer, a way to draw the daimyo's troops into battle at a spot of Godo's choosing. Hidetsugu well knew the problems faced by the sanzoku each winter, and he also knew that Godo would not be able to pass up such an opportunity.

The warlord prodded his yak and rode down the ridge toward Hidetsugu. Like all sane creatures, he feared and respected the ogre's power, but he had no reason to expect an attack. Their dealings had been few in number, but they were on good terms. If Hidetsugu wanted him dead, he would have used brute force, not guile.

"Hail, warlord of the Sokenzan." Hidetsugu was wearing a dusty red robe with metal plates across his shoulders and chest. He seemed calm, even thoughtful.

Godo stiffened his back. "Hail, Hidetsugu of the o-bake-mono." Even from atop his steed, the towering bandit chief had to tilt his head back to address the ogre. "You have something to trade?"

"I have something to give." The ogre reached into a small pack on the ground beside him and drew out a black disk with blue markings.

"Break this seal in a place where you want to catch Konda's attention," he said. "It will draw the daimyo's troops and help you destroy them."

Godo looked closely at the disk, squinting his eyes under his thick brow. When he saw the markings clearly, his eyes opened wide. Beneath him, the yak snorted, reacting to his anxiety.

"I refuse, noble ogre. That is the mark of the yuki-onna. I would never unleash something like that at ground level. I am surprised you even suggest it."

Hidetsugu smiled, displaying his curved teeth. "This is the spirit from the Heart of Frost. She has been compelled by a gifted kanji magician. The daimyo's troops will see whomever they wish to rescue most. When they approach her, they will die." He offered the disk. "The Heart of Frost is no longer cursed, but the curse itself goes on. You must choose where it will strike next, and wisely, so that your people will benefit."

Godo shook his head. "Too dangerous. How will I get rid of her once she's released?"

"You won't need to. By her nature, she is tied to the land itself. You simply have to keep your tribe out of her new hunting ground, the way you kept them away from the Heart of Frost."

"So all I need to do is turn a perfectly safe patch of ground into a haunted killing field. Again, I refuse."

"Don't be hasty," Hidetsugu said. He leaned down, whispering conspiratorially. "This is a rare opportunity. Konda's army has never been so small or so inexperienced. You can occupy a significant number of his border patrol with this single spell. You can station warriors on the edges of her territory and pick off any who make it through. In less than a month, the border will be as good as undefended.

"Think how effective your secret assault on Eiganjo will be when combined with this gambit. Think how well your myojin will reward you. And if it pleases you," he added, "think how grateful I will be if you accept my help.

"Of course, I would be duty bound to help transport the yuki-onna back to her mountain once your victory had been achieved. There is no risk to you, great warlord, and much reward."

Godo stared at the ogre's huge, leering face. He did not trust Hidetsugu, but he could see the wisdom of his words. Konda had never been so vulnerable. Staggered by the Kami War and new trouble on the border, an akki assault on his capital might topple him completely.

"I have your word that you'll help remove her?"

"May Chaos take my eyes if I do not. Recall, bandit. I have no love for Konda, and the Sokenzan is my home, too." The ogre's wild eyes were inches away, and Godo's head spun under Hidetsugu's hot breath.

"Come, mighty Godo. Release the cold beast, and let her run rampant. When she is gorged on your enemy, we will subdue her once more and march her back to the Heart of Frost. I can even guarantee that the same kanji mage who snared her will return to do it again."

Hidetsugu proffered the disk, holding it flat on his palm in front of Godo's eyes. The warlord glanced at the ogre, then at the plate, then closed his eyes.

"Done," he said. He reached out and took the black seal with both hands.

"You honor me." Hidetsugu rose to his full height. "I will return to my valley. Send a rider if you need me. Remember to break the seal in a place where Konda's troops will see the result. Then withdraw until you are sure how far her influence extends."

The ogre bowed, and turned to leave.

"Hidetsugu!"

Without turning, the o-bakemono stopped.

"How far do you suppose she'll wander?" Godo turned the disk over in his hands.

Hidetsugu craned his head. "I do not know," he said, "but if Konda sends enough men, it will be easy to tell."

Godo grinned. "I think I know just the spot."

* * * * *

Back in the confines of his cavern, Hidetsugu tossed off his metal plates and the red robe beneath them. He clapped his hands once, lighting every torch and brazier in the cavern.

He strode across the floor, muttering and grumbling to himself. Near the shrine to his oni was a pile of jagged metal pieces and a gigantic spiked tetsubo club. Calmly, deliberately, Hidetsugu strapped the brass-colored plates onto his shoulders, elbows, and hips. He lifted the tetsubo and swung it viciously through the air in front of him. He nodded at the sound it made, pleased with the club's heft and feel.

His armor clanging as he walked, Hidetsugu strode to the center of his home and rested the tetsubo on the floor. He clapped his hands again and called out, "Come to me, my children."

The sound of sandaled feet came from the far corner of the cavern. Eight cold-eyed yamabushi walked across the cavern in tight formation. When they reached Hidetsugu, they formed a semicircle around him and dropped to one knee.

Hidetsugu appraised them like a horse trader. They were all lean, muscular, and graceful. They wore their fresh scars and burns without complaint. Their expressions differed—some were blank and inscrutable, some were dour and dangerous, and a few wore wide-eyed expressions of feral glee. All of their eyes were the same, however: cold, distant, and without the slightest spark of life.

The o-bakemono nodded. He had trained them well.

"You were trained to battle kami," he said. "You were instructed in the ancient and secret arts of the yamabushi to defend your homes in these troubled times.

"However, warriors should not wait for battle. They should march out and seek it. Your former masters were cowards, frightened to teach you anything that they themselves could not control. They are dead now, and I will complete your education.

"Come with me now, destroyers of kami. We have bloody work to do."

Silent, the eight yamabushi stood as one and fell back into their ranks behind Hidetsugu. The ogre didn't mind. He liked a good battle roar, but what his students lacked in volume, they made up for in determination.

Hidetsugu grinned. Yes, indeed. He had trained them well.

* * * * *

Godo and three of his lieutenants stood overlooking the northern border with Towabara. The foothills below were broken up by a series of natural rock formations and jagged piles of boulders. Beyond the stones was an expanse of dry, flat land, then a small rise to a hill covered in scrub grass. It was a dull and deserted place, but once it had been one of the most traveled routes between the mountains and Konda's realm.

Three mounted sentries from Konda's cavalry sat on top of the hill opposite the bandits. They were not there to fight but to summon a larger body of troops if the sanzoku started to mass or tried to cross the border. Konda's generals had grown conservative. They were not willing to start a fight, but they were ready to finish one.

"Withdraw," said Godo. Most of his subordinates immediately turned and headed back into the hinterlands, but one stayed behind.

"Go," Godo said. "They couldn't reach me here, even with their most powerful bows."

The bandit officer nodded. "But their archers go mounted, great one. If they closed the gap on horseback—"

"They'll never get the chance." Godo smiled and jerked his head. "Go on. I'll be right behind you."

He waited until the lieutenant had vanished from view then turned back to the sentries. Indifferent, they watched him as he opened his pack and withdrew the black seal.

"From our ancestors, Konda." He raised the tablet high, then drew his arm back. "May your tower fall with you inside."

Godo hurled the seal like a discus high over the rocky expanse. The sentries watched it arc gracefully down until it disappeared among the rocks. From his closer position, Godo heard the ceramic seal break. He calculated the distance at roughly one hundred yards.

A stiff, bitter breeze swept up from the foothills, and Godo repressed a shudder. On the other side, he saw Konda's sentries lose control of their horses for a moment. When they had calmed their steeds, both men gathered their cloaks around them and hunched their shoulders.

One of the sentries pointed, excitedly prodding his partner. The second sentry looked and nodded, quickly taking on the first sentry's excitement.

Godo glanced down among the rocks. There, standing stiffly on the cold hard ground, was a female figure. Even from here, Godo could see she was tall and beautiful in her gleaming white robes. Her head was tilted forward so that her hair fell around her face. The woman turned her veiled face from side to side then stood upright, tossing her head back. She stared up at

Godo, locking her empty black eyes on his. Cold terror gripped his spine, but Godo held the woman's gaze and nodded. She did not nod back.

Half-hypnotized, Godo forced himself to turn away. He knew he should not stare, should not look into those terrible eyes at all now that she had seen him, but he desperately wanted to. He wanted to let her look him full in the face, to embrace the terrible cold that crept through his guts.

Instead, Godo placed the back of his hand across his eyes and went down the hillside, putting bare rock between his eyes and those of the snow woman. As he did, he caught one last glimpse of the sentries on the far hill. Instead of shielding their eyes, they were gesturing and pointing, trying to catch the woman's attention.

Don't worry, Godo thought as he ran. She'll come to you soon.

He wondered how the sentries' commanding officer would react when they told him. He wondered how fast it would take the news to travel up the chain of command, from the border back into Towabara, all the way into Eiganjo and the daimyo's tower.

He wondered how they would tell Konda that his daughter, Princess Michiko herself, had been spotted on the frontier, within throwing distance of Godo's army.

CHAPTER 10

Toshi was forced to kneel before Boss Uramon. This time he was in chains with no less than four of Kiku's flowers squirming on his torso. The ochimusha kept his eyes downcast, even as Marrow-Gnawer prodded him with a stick and capered behind him.

"So," Uramon said. "You have returned." She stood once more in the center of her enclosure of black sand and stones. "I no longer wish to hire you, Toshi. That ship has sailed."

Toshi slowly looked up. He sighed heavily.

"Damn," he said. "I was just starting to get tired of thinking for myself, too. You sure there's nothing I can do for you?"

Uramon shook her head, her pallid face like wax. "You can die, ochimusha. You are talented but not worth the trouble. You're barely worth the six hatchet men it cost me to bring you back here."

Toshi smiled. "And a handful of nezumi. If we're balancing our accounts, let's be thorough."

"Kiku," Uramon said. "Have our guest suspended from the manor's front gate. Wait until I take my seat on the second-floor balcony overlooking the courtyard before you activate your blooms. I want to watch him strain as the life leaves him."

"Forgive me, Boss. I can't do that."

A ripple of annoyance crossed Uramon's passive face. "I must have misheard you, dear. What?"

Toshi quickly scanned the chamber, noting the position of Uramon's guards. She was taking no chances this time, even with Toshi chained and festooned with camellias. There were ten hatchet men in the room, four more outside the main door, and a half-dozen nezumi scattered around the hallways.

"Things became . . . complicated in the mountains." Kiku stepped out from behind Toshi so that there was nothing between herself and Uramon. "In order to acquire Toshi and bring him here, I had to make concessions."

"Concessions? What kind of concessions? I authorized no—"

"This kind." As she spoke, Kiku drew her throwing axe and hurled it into the nearest guard's chest. The man grunted and dropped to his knees, a confused expression on his face.

Marrow-Gnawer screeched as he brought his short staff down on Toshi's back. The weak link they had used to hold his chains in place shattered, and black metal scraps jingled like coins as they rained down on Uramon's floor. Marrow handed Toshi his jitte, turned, and buried his staff in the midsection of an approaching nezumi footpad.

The purple flowers on Toshi's chest dropped away, withering as they fell. Kiku had not imbued them with any special magic other than enough animation to look as if they were alive.

"Kill them." Uramon's monotonous voice did not even rise when issuing death warrants. In fact, she sounded almost bored.

Her actions belied her tone, however, as she quickly crossed the sand pit toward the side door.

Toshi grinned. He knew where that door led. He didn't dare give Uramon enough time to reach the secret chamber in the basement, but first he had to help his fellow reckoners clear the room.

It had been a while since he'd seen Kiku or Marrow in action. Now, in the thick of this brawl with Uramon's henchmen, he remembered why it was so important to surround himself with people who could fight.

Marrow-Gnawer was especially impressive, if only because a single nezumi was rarely a serious threat. But Marrow was a chieftain, a leader among his tribe, and he had earned his position by being tougher and nastier than the other rats. They all fought dirty, but Marrow fought with a special kind of savagery, raking eyes with his filthy, ragged claws, kicking groins with his pointed toes, ripping chunks of flesh off the other nezumi with his black and broken teeth.

Six against one was too much even for the strongest rat warrior, so Toshi slid into the confusion and rammed his jitte into the back of a rat that had taken hold of Marrow-Gnawer's tail. He then drew his weapon and dragged the bloody tip across the face of a second nezumi aggressor. Toshi held the vermin's rusty blade at bay with his free hand as he quickly completed a pestilence kanji on the rat-man's face.

Once the symbol was complete, the stricken rat choked and clawed at his own throat. Thick black boils erupted across his face. As he opened his mouth to gasp for air, Toshi saw similar pustules on his tongue and the inside of his mouth. His stomach bulged, and his eyes rolled back as he toppled. He collided with two more of his fellow nezumi on the way down, and soon they too were writhing in boil-covered agony on the floor. Seconds later, their struggles ceased.

Toshi was impressed. Nezumi blood was especially potent for this kind of spell, but he hadn't expected a reaction like this.

The remaining rats struck at Marrow again and again. While he was only slightly larger than they, their blows had no effect whatsoever. Marrow himself was the only one who seemed to be doing damage, and soon the entire tangle of screeching, biting rats was covered in blood, clumps of hair, and broken teeth. The last of Uramon's nezumi dropped his cudgel and fell to his knees, begging Marrow for mercy. Marrow-Gnawer staved the side of the beggar's skull with his staff and kicked him in the throat as he fell.

Toshi glanced over at Kiku. She had retrieved her axe and was standing among a small pile of dead men, each with a purple flower digging into his chest. Eight more of Uramon's hatchet men had surrounded her, but none was willing to engage, having seen what she was capable of.

"Marrow," Toshi said. "You and Kiku have to handle this from here. I'm going after the boss."

"I don't need his help!" Kiku broke a guard's nose with the flat of her axe then dropped and chopped off the front half of his foot. The man screamed once before Kiku shoved a camellia in his mouth. She spun him around and ducked behind him as two of the guards' axes slammed into his body.

"Help her anyway," Toshi said to the nezumi. "Just don't get too close."

Marrow-Gnawer looked unconvinced, but he nodded.

Toshi concentrated, feeling the scar on his forearm. He saw the Myojin of Night's Reach in his mind's eye, and he called upon her power. Instead of fading away, however, he held the magic in reserve and rushed toward Uramon's side door. He ran straight across the black sand pit, marring its peaceful whorls and lines, kicking stones from his path and tracking sand on the lacquered wood floor.

He kicked the closed door with all of his weight and momentum. Beyond the doorway, a stairwell led down into a dark and silent cellar.

Dark and silent, Toshi thought. Perfect. He smiled, and relaxed his mind, accepting the myojin's blessing.

Before his body had completely faded away, Toshi leaped out over the darkened stairway, floating like a ghost until he faded from view.

* * * * *

Uramon moved very quickly for a woman her age. She had never been a warrior, but she was tenacious and smart enough to control her corner of Takenuma's illegal community in the shadow of the daimyo's own tower. Through frequent go-yo crackdowns and the expanding strife of the Kami War, Uramon had not just survived but prospered.

As she picked her way through the darkened recesses below her manor, Uramon calculated. She had assembled enough guards to contain Toshi, but not Toshi and Kiku. By now they had probably killed or incapacitated all of the hatchet men and nezumi in her meditation chamber.

However, by now word had almost certainly spread that the boss was under attack, and her more formidable bodyguards and retainers would be rushing in to earn their keep. All she had to do was stay out of harm's way until the rest of her manor guards completed the task of killing Toshi. She hoped Kiku survived, for then Uramon would own the jushi for life. Her clan elders would never have approved their prize student's behavior and would surely abandon her rather than seek further conflict with Uramon. The boss's thin lips crinkled as she flirted with the beginnings of a smile. She relished the thought of Kiku's pride tearing the jushi apart over the years it would take to make amends for this night.

Uramon paused, listening closely and peering through the dim light. Satisfied, she felt for a hidden lever in the wall. Next to the lever was a small socket. Uramon made a fist and slotted her ring into the socket, a perfect fit, then pulled the lever forward.

A section of the wall silently fell into the floor. Uramon darted inside and pulled a matching lever, and the wall rose, sealing the entrance.

Her secret passage was known to no one but herself, and she kept one of her most powerful assets hidden within. The architects who constructed this passage and the laborers who transported the asset were all dead. This section of the manor was kept in almost complete darkness, and anyone caught venturing near the stairs would be ground up, dried, and spread across Uramon's sand garden.

The boss felt for a candle that was kept in a sconce on the wall. She took it down and lit it, holding its pale weak flame aloft as she crept along the passage. Her immobile features did not change as she walked, but her eyes grew wider and more animated.

At its end the passage opened up into a small circular alcove. The candle revealed small sections of a large silk tapestry, but Uramon knew every detail by heart without seeing it. The tapestry showed a tall, black-hooded figure with a gleaming white porcelain mask. She was surrounded by pale, emaciated hands that circled her like a flock of birds.

Before the tapestry was a sturdy oaken chest of drawers. On top of the chest stood several lit candles arranged around a silver plate. A strange artifact rested on the plate. It was just over a foot high, with two piles of square stones flanking a black metal portcullis. Fine silver filigree connected the two square columns over the portcullis, with an elegant symbol woven through in flat black iron. Uramon glanced down at her fist and saw the same symbol on her ring below the flickering light of the candle.

"This must be the Shadow Gate."

Uramon dropped the candle and quickly backed up until she touched the wall. Toshi's voice had come from behind her, near the passageway. It was impossible for him to be here, but she heard his voice just the same.

"Are you really here, Toshi?" she called, "or is this some common *mahotsukai* magic trick?" With her hands thrust deep into the sleeves of her robe, Uramon slid the poisoned needle from its sheath on her arm.

"I'm here, Boss." The ochimusha's voice came from the right side of the room. "I had heard you kept a shrine to the Myojin of Night's Reach in your cellar. Have I mentioned that I'm a believer myself?"

The candle still burned on the floor, but it was dying quickly. The candles on the chest of drawers were adequate for lighting up the artifact on the plate, but they did not help illuminate the room. Uramon narrowed her eyes and tried to pinpoint Toshi's location by sound.

"A believer in what?" Uramon kept her arms wrapped tightly around herself, the long needle ready in her hand. "And who told you this?"

"The Myojin of Night's Reach," Toshi said, from the left side of the chamber. "And the Smiling Kami of the Crescent Moon. I don't think he meant to tell me, he was just making conversation."

Uramon spared a quick glance at the tapestry. The image was indeed of the Myojin of Night's Reach, and the Shadow Gate below it drew its power from her. Uramon gritted her teeth in the darkness. Toshi's greatest strength and his greatest weakness had always been his refusal to subordinate himself to one of the major kami. If now he had, as he claimed, the ochimusha was even more unpredictable and dangerous.

Uramon relaxed her grip but maintained her hold on the needle. She took a slow step toward the artifact on the plate.

Toshi's voice was very close to her, but moving all the while as he spoke.

"Ahh," he said. "This is where things come to head, boss. You want to use the Gate to escape . . . possibly to a place where there are more guards and fewer disobedient former reckoners.

"But I also want the Gate. I need it for the next step in my spiritual evolution."

Uramon's temper flared, both at Toshi's sarcastic tone and the suggestion that he would relieve her of her property. Her voice, however, remained dull and monotonous. "The Shadow Gate is mine," she droned. She took another step toward it. "It is for my use only. You have neither the skill nor the knowledge to employ it safely."

"Worried about my welfare?" Toshi mocked. "Thank you, Boss, but I'm no longer your employee. Let me worry about me."

Uramon took another step. She was nearly there. "I care not at all for you, Toshi. I just want you to understand there's no profit in stealing the Gate, or even trying to use it. It will not function for you."

"Not without the right preparations," Toshi said. "And your ring."

Uramon drew the poisoned needle with one hand an lunged for the artifact with the other. She drove her clenched fist with the ring extended directly at the center of the silver filigree.

A numbing wave of cold surged through Uramon, and she felt the air around her thicken. She still strained with all her might to reach the chest of drawers, but she could see her hand inching forward, slowing, stopping as if there were five stout men holding her back. Her breath clouded in front of her eyes, and stabbing pain shot up her arms and legs.

Uramon fell heavily to the floor, her outstretched fist mere inches from the chest of drawers. The long needle snapped in two beneath her falling body, but luckily she did not stick herself with the pointed end.

She could not move. She could not speak. She could only lie still in this prone position with one arm twisted beneath her and the other failing to reach the Shadow Gate. Her view of the secret chamber was tilted ninety degrees, so that the floor was the wall and the wall was the floor.

Toshi strode out of the darkness. A purple-black kanji had appeared on his forehead, and while Uramon was extremely learned, she did not recognize the symbol. It seemed to be a combination of the kanji for "frigid," a second symbol she didn't recognize, and Toshi's own hyozan triangle.

The bruise-colored kanji pulsated. Uramon felt a fresh wave of numbness cross her entire body. She blinked tiny crystals of ice from her eyes.

With practiced motions, Toshi turned her over and removed the pieces of poisoned needle. He lifted her wrist and gently pried the ring from her finger.

"This ring," he said, "allows you to employ the Myojin's power. The Shadow Gate contains that power, keeping it in check until you need it." Toshi dropped the ring next to Uramon's face and crushed it beneath his sandal.

"Shadow is an aspect of Night," Toshi intoned. "And I am an acolyte of Shadow." He stepped forward and lifted the stone-and-metal artifact off the plate. "This power now belongs to me."

A moan escaped Uramon's blue lips. Without the ring, the Gate was worthless to her. If Toshi tried to use it, he would either be consumed or sent to some unimaginably distant place, perhaps even arriving with his insides outside.

Spitefully, she moaned again, trying to infuse her cries with panic and desperation. If Toshi thought she didn't want him to use the gate, he was almost certain to do so. Once he did, she would have time to thaw and summon help.

But Toshi ignored her. His plans, whatever their final goal, included seizing the Shadow Gate immediately.

With the artifact in his hands, Toshi smiled and bowed at Uramon. The silver metal began to glow as the black symbol woven through it absorbed the light like sand absorbs water.

Toshi held the Shadow Gate in both hands as the glow slowly spread across his body. As the symbol drew in the glow back in, it also absorbed Toshi and the Gate itself.

The last thing Uramon saw before the room went black was the ochimusha's cruel smile, and his wide, expectant eyes.

Then the cold claimed her and Uramon fell into a death-like sleep.

CHAPTER 11

Toshi went from standing in Uramon's rapidly chilling basement to hurtling through a sightless, soundless void like a leaf
on a river. There was no breeze to stir his hair, no landscape
whizzing by, but there was a overwhelming sense of forward
motion. He could not see where he was going, but he was going
there very quickly.

This must be travel by shadow, he thought. He was fairly certain no one had used the Gate's power for many years now, not
even Uramon. The stories about her said she had some unknown
method of eliminating her rivals that allowed her to seize control
of things in and around the Araba, but that had been quite some
time ago, in Toshi's youth. Now, as a worshipper of Night, the
power was his alone.

His immeasurable momentum eased, slowing to the point
where Toshi felt he was floating instead of flying. The formless
void around him remained the same, but his motion through it
had definitely changed. As he drifted, he realized that he had
felt something like this before, when he'd been stricken down
by snakefolk venom and his oath-brother Kobo was being
drowned.

He wished he could have learned the mechanism Uramon employed to select a destination. It had something to do with her ring, he was sure, but the ring was made for Uramon alone. It tied her to the Shadow Gate, reserving it for her exclusive use and communicating her goals to the magical force that powered it.

Toshi drifted to what felt like a complete stop. He hung suspended in the void as the first true misgivings about this endeavor stirred in his brain. Without the ring, he had no way of directing his passage. He expected his first blind jaunt to send him somewhere familiar, some place from a memory so clear and sharp that he wouldn't have to navigate. Instead, he seemed to have completed only half a journey with no way to complete or abandon it.

Toshi turned his head in the darkness, scanning for any sight or sound that could help orient him. The other spells he had invoked with the Myojin of Night's Reach had all been intuitive, almost instinctual actions. As he'd been trained, he assessed the situation and then fell back on the vast vocabulary of kanji spells he'd assembled. It was an improvisational art that so far had merged well enough with the structured worship of a major kami.

Wresting control of the Shadow Gate from Uramon should have been no more difficult than trapping the yuki-onna's essence—which, he could admit to himself, was far more difficult and painful than he would ever let on. But he had done that under especially trying circumstances, and he refused to accept that a jaunt through the Shadow Gate was more of a challenge than yoking the curse that wandered the Heart of Frost.

Toshi pondered as he floated like a bubble in oil. Perhaps he was guilty of falling into his old habits, of trying to accomplish everything himself without beseeching his patron kami. He pictured her once more, imagining her as she had been on Uramon's secret tapestry, a field of fine black fabric and a bone-white mask surrounded by disembodied hands.

"Hear me, Myojin of Night's Reach." Toshi's voice was soundless in the void, but he felt the vibration of his words in his jaw and his ears. "I am alone, helpless, lost. Guide your servant home."

A few moments passed. Then, Toshi winced as the kanji on his body began to seethe and sting. The hyozan mark on his wrist, the kanji on his forearm that allowed him to disappear, and the bruise-colored symbol on his forehead all throbbed in unison.

Look up. The whispering voice was soft but somehow vast, bypassing Toshi's ears and stabbing directly into his brain. Though he had only heard it on one occasion, it was impossible not to recognize the myojin's voice.

Toshi looked. The view remained the same, that is, no view at all, but Toshi felt waves of force gathering beneath him. Like an insect in a child's cupped hands, Toshi was taken up, rising with ever-increasing speed.

A speck of white appeared on the horizon, a point no bigger than a distant star on a cloudy night. It remained there for several long seconds before it started to expand.

Toshi's speed increased further, pressing the skin against his skull. The white dot grew larger, swelling to fill more and more of the dark void as Toshi rushed toward it. The brightness burned his eyes, and he closed them, but he could still see the glow beyond his eyelids. He felt his body coming apart. He screamed, but the sheer velocity carried his voice away and rendered him mute.

Toshi opened his eyes just as he hit the field of white. The small speck had expanded to fill the entire void, and as he crossed through the border from darkness to light, the change in his surroundings hit his entire body like a slap from a giant hand.

Toshi's own scream caught up with him as gravity brutally yanked him down to the ground. He grunted and landed heavily on his stomach.

Toshi paused. Ground? He felt around with his hands, still blind and partially deaf, confirming the surface beneath him. Yes, there it was. He was on solid rock, or at least a well-built floor. This new world was only a mass of formless white to his eyes, he at least he was no longer trapped in the void of shadows. There was solid ground beneath him and a slight breeze on his face. He had been admitted to the myojin's *honden*, her inner sanctum and place of power.

Rise, acolyte of Shadow. So you have declared yourself, so you shall be.

Toshi cracked his eyes open. The white glare had faded back to a dull silver glow. Before him stood the Myojin of Night's Reach in all her glory.

A black curtain of luxurious fabric spread twenty feet wide and fifteen feet high. A pair of emaciated arms stretched out over the top of the curtain, suspending the fabric like a grotesque curtain rod. The myojin's smooth white mask was at the center of the black field, framed by the swirling sheets of darkness. If Toshi squinted, he could see the outline of her hood and robes, though they seemed to merge and separate from the curtain at random as it billowed behind her. Her attendant disembodied hands floated above and to the side of the curtain, palms forward and fingers pointing straight up. The scene was deathly silent until Toshi spoke, his voice bright.

"Hello there," he called. "Did you bring me here, or did I take a wrong turn?"

You have been busy, the great kami's voice came. *Isolating aspects of our power and claiming them for your own use.*

"I've never been one to take half-steps," Toshi admitted, "when leaping in with both feet will get me there faster."

I salute your alacrity. You have acquired access to the Shadow Gate. What will you do with it?

"That depends on how far it can take me."

As its name implies, it is a gateway through the realm of shadows. Anywhere that light exists but is partially obscured will now be open to you.

"Anywhere? No matter what locks or wards or sentries are in place?"

Anywhere. But go carefully, my acolyte. It will take you past any boundary, but it cannot protect you once you arrive.

Toshi grinned. "Not an issue, really. But thank you for the warning." He glanced around at the strange, half-visible sur-roundings. "Tell me, O Night, did Uramon also come here when she first used the Gate?"

She did. Though she was better informed about its function, and she came with a mechanism for restricting its use. Also, she was far more humble in my presence.

"So the Gate is mine now?"

It is.

Toshi bowed. "Another blessing, gratefully received. I honor you, Myojin."

Do you? I wonder. How long will you continue to exploit my gifts without the slightest offer of payment?

Toshi's grin hardened. "I expected this to come up sooner

or later. You have been very generous, O Night. What could a
humble ochimusha offer in return?"

The shadow chamber was silent for so long Toshi began to
wonder if he'd receive an answer. Then, the myojin's voice came
again.

Like you, she said, *I choose to leave my options open. But I
am comforted by the act of offering.*

Toshi was a good deal less comforted by the myojin's interest
in open-ended compensation, but he kept his feelings to himself.
"You have but to ask," he said, thinking, I'm sure we can come
to an arrangement.

*You interest me, Toshi Umezawa. If you took the time to plan
more, you would not risk so much. Yet if you were not so bold,
you would not accomplish so much. It is no wonder that Mochi
brought you to me. I believe you are the first being from the
utsushiyo to have confounded his expectations.*

Toshi cocked his head. "I have questions about that one," he
said. "May I impose upon your giving nature a while longer?"

*I think not. You have acquired three aspects of Shadow so
far, plus the use of the Gate. You are in a much better position to
confirm or dismiss your concerns about Mochi than I am. Even
now, you do not fully trust the great spirits of the kakuriyo.*

"It's hard to cast off the habit of a lifetime."

*Go now, Toshi Umezawa, and take this with you: Mochi seeks
to save your world and ours, but only on his specific terms. Think
carefully about your true allegiances and cling to them. Only
this will see you through the coming maelstrom.*

The curtain behind the myojin began to withdraw into itself,
shrinking up into the cadaverous arms above.

Toshi called, "And what of your interests, O Night? If you

have a purpose for me, state it, and I will see it through to the best of my abilities."

The myojin's frozen mask seemed to smile. Perhaps it was the dry amusement of her voice, but Toshi definitely had the sense she was entertained.

Perhaps, she said. *Or perhaps you would use that information to plan a counter-strategy that would leave me as bereft and beaten as Uramon.*

Toshi tried to look shocked. "Never, O Night. I am your humble—"

You are many things, ochimusha, but humble is not one of them. She had stopped her withdrawal so that only her mask and the hood around it remained. There was still a cluster of floating hands above and behind her.

Here, she said. The empty eyes in the white mask flashed, and black light spilled out of them. Toshi felt something fall away from his body, like he had shed a portion of his skin.

Now the item known as the Shadow Gate is no more. Its power has been transmitted to you, Toshi. Your body is now capable of transporting itself, so that no one may do to you what you have done to Uramon.

Toshi glanced down. There was an uncomfortable sensation on his chest, as if some caustic worm were wriggling just below the surface of his skin. Hesitantly, he pulled open his shirt to reveal a jet-black kanji forming on the center of his breastbone, the same symbol that had been woven through the filigree on Uramon's artifact.

"Uh . . . thank you, O Night."

Go forth, my acolyte. Use the power I have given you and the power you have taken. Know that I am with you always.

With a sudden slurping sound, the black fabric quickly drew in upon itself and the white mask faded away.

Toshi stood for a few moments. He absently closed his shirt and laid his open palm across the new kanji on his chest.

Without the myojin to sustain it, the solid bubble he was occupying began to decay. In a matter of minutes, he would be floating aimlessly on the void once more.

Toshi pressed his hand into his chest. He cleared his mind and pictured the secret chamber where he had left Uramon.

Something much louder than his heart thumped beneath his hand, and Toshi disappeared.

* * * * *

Toshi felt his body temperature plummet as he regained both form and weight. A thin layer of frost had formed on the walls of Uramon's hidden treasure trove. The chest of drawers and the silver plate were dusted with white, and the tapestry depicting the myojin creaked stiffly as Toshi moved through the room.

Boss Uramon was gone, which was not a hopeful sign. Toshi blew on his hands, watching the skin of ice spread across the walls and floor. It was well past time to leave.

With an effort, he pried his feet from the floor with a harsh cracking sound—the ice had begun to crawl up the edges of his sandals. He would have been content to test the new power his myojin had granted him, but first he should check up on Marrow-Gnawer and Kiku. Toshi was confident they were alive because the hyozan mark on his hand had not throbbed or burned as it would have if they'd been killed, but just because the weren't dead yet didn't mean he could abandon them. All he needed right now was another reckoning to distract him from the matter at hand.

Toshi quickly exited the passage and dashed up the staircase to Uramon's meditation chamber. He felt the temperature rise slightly as he rose, but it was still cold enough to be a hazard, and growing cold enough to kill.

There were more bodies in the chamber now than before, but a quick examination showed that none belonged to his fellow reckoners. In the gathering cold, the corpses were stiffening more quickly than normal.

Where were the rest of Uramon's guards, he wondered. He knew that along with her small army of hatchet men and indentured nezumi, the boss kept enslaved monsters, hungry *gaki* ghosts with grasping hands and featureless faces, even toxic *akuba* with multiple arms and forked tongues. Where were these more monstrous retainers?

Toshi carefully opened the outer door that led from the meditation chamber to the main hall. He whistled softly, white fog pouring between his pursed lips.

The hallway floor was littered with frozen corpses—human, nezumi, and monster alike. They all seemed to have fallen in mid-charge, weapons drawn, claws extended, snarls of rage on their faces. Toshi prodded a nearby hatchet man with his toe, and the frozen thug's ear broke off like the tip of an icicle.

"Okay, then." Toshi wrapped his arms around himself and headed for the front door. The huge half-ogre who guarded the door leaned against the nearest wall, propped upright like a half-felled tree.

Then Toshi was through the door and out into the warm, wet air of the swamp. It was foul-smelling and thick with buzzing flies and biting moths, but it was a far cry from the increasingly brutal cold inside Uramon's manor.

"What in the name of the cold gray hell did you do in there?"

Kiku stood at the far end of the path, just inside Uramon's exterior gate. She appeared uninjured as she casually sniffed a camellia pinned to her cloak.

Beside her on the ground lay Boss Uramon. In death, Numai's criminal overlord had thrown off the passive façade she wore in life but only with the help of one of Kiku's flowers. A single purple bloom sprouted from the center of Uramon's powdered forehead, its thorny roots dug deep into her skull. Below the camellia, Uramon's face was twisted into a mask of pain and fury, her teeth bared, her lips stretched tight, and her tongue protruding.

Toshi gestured. "Why'd you kill the Boss?"

"Why didn't you? I don't know what you've got planned for the immediate future, but none of us would have lasted another week with a vengeful Uramon on the loose." Kiku gestured to the manor. "Answer your own question. Why'd you kill everyone else?"

Toshi turned. Uramon's splendid house was surrounded by a thickening bank of white fog. It didn't seem to be expanding past the walls of the manor, but it was growing more opaque all the time.

"I was just showing off," he lied. "As you said, it's better to end this little drama here. No survivors means no sequel." He looked around the empty courtyard. "Where's Marrow?"

"He's alive," Kiku said, "but he lit out as soon as the cold started to claim the others. You're lucky we were both able to walk. If we'd been trapped in there, you'd have killed your own reckoners." Her eyes narrowed, and she smiled savagely. "From what I'm told, that wouldn't be too healthy for you."

Toshi nodded. "It's pretty much the standard blood boiling, throat closing, and eyes bursting that comes with many broken oaths. Only when one hyozan turns on another, the others are also compelled to action. The idea was to keep the betrayer immobile and agonized until Hidetsugu or myself could come settle things properly."

Kiku sneered. "So it's a good thing all around we didn't die. No thanks to you."

"I have extraordinary trust in you," Toshi said.

Kiku tossed her head, unimpressed.

"But I also have a piece of advice. Return to your clan, or at least some place where you can lie low. This—" he waved his arms around to include the frozen manor and the dead Boss—"will stir things up for awhile. Others will move in once they realize Uramon has fallen. You'll want to stay out of the way until things settle down. I'm sure you'll find an agreeable position with the new Boss, whoever that turns out to be."

Kiku straightened her cloak and began lacing it shut. "I don't need to you to coach me, oath-brother."

"Actually, you do. I left Uramon alive because I thought removing her would help the soratami. They're muscling in on her territory, remember?"

"What is that to me?"

"It's a matter of great concern. The moonfolk have the best assassins, the sneakiest shinobi, the toughest warriors. Without Uramon, they probably will take over here or at least lay claim to a major chunk of the market. *You must not work for them*, jushi. Not even as a freelancer."

Kiku's face grew red. "Why not? Who are you to tell—"

"The soratami are my enemy," Toshi said evenly. "More, they are connected to the academy, which is connected to the death of Hidetsugu's apprentice. There could be a serious conflict if a hyozan reckoner took work with people the hyozan is targeting." He shook his head. "Bad business."

Kiku sniffed. "More boiling blood?"

"Maybe. I was thinking specifically of Hidetsugu peeling you like a piece of overripe fruit. Do not ally yourself with anyone remotely associated with moon kami. It's going to be a rough winter for them."

Kiku stared at Toshi, hate in her eyes, but she nodded, slowly, and only once.

"And you?" she said. "What will you do next? Where will you go?"

"I don't actually know," Toshi said. He slapped his chest. "I think the answer is: anywhere I want."

CHAPTER 12

Princess Michiko sat at her writing desk, staring wistfully out into the smoke and haze that had settled over Eiganjo. From her window in the tall tower, the murky mist below was like a permanent fog. She heard the sounds of battle daily as hostile kami manifested and were met by either her father's army or the great spirit dragon Yosei.

The magical serpent had halted the kami onslaught, even if he could not turn the tide and drive them away from her father's final stronghold. Yosei was truly a blessing from the spirit world, and he fought ferociously for the preservation of her people. She knew the daimyo had powerful mages working for him and had seen him involved in complicated rituals, but the depth of his power never ceased to amaze her. Had he been so great before he violated the spirit world, or was his majesty due primarily to the power he'd stolen?

Each day, Michiko's thoughts went back to the vision Mochi had shown to her. Her father, flanked by master wizards from Minamo academy and mysterious advisors from the soratami, had punched a hole in the barrier between the physical world and the spirit realm. With his own hands, he had reached in and drawn something out, something so vast and inscrutable that the entire kakuriyo had reacted instantly. Daimyo Konda had disturbed the most dangerous hornet's nest imaginable, and his nation and his people had been bearing the stings ever since. If not for the power he commanded . . .

Isamaru, her father's trusted dog, grumbled on the floor beside her. The huge, cream-colored Akita was over ten years old, but he was still spry and strong enough to take down a fully armored soldier. Konda had lavished attention on the dog when it was a puppy, but as the years went by the Kami War intensified and the daimyo spent more and more time with the thing he had taken. Bereft of their kindly paternal figure, Michiko and Isamaru had found each other, and a strong friendship had taken root.

She welcomed the big dog's company. It had taken weeks for her father to acknowledge her requests for Isamaru, and even longer for him to grant it. She suspected that General Takeno, first among her father's officers, had allowed the dog to visit her in the tower. An old soldier like her father, Takeno at least had not forgotten the simple joys of a loyal dog.

She reached down and lightly scratched Isamaru's ribcage. He thumped his tail appreciatively. As much as she hated her captivity, Isamaru loved it. He had nothing to do all day but be with Michiko and enjoy her frequent attention.

There had been no reply from Toshi, Riko, or any of the other messenger kanji she'd sent. Perhaps she had been using the wrong symbol or inscribing it incorrectly. The first few days were the hardest, as each passing bird and breeze brought her breathless to the window. Now, weeks after she had sent the last messenger, Michiko had all but given up hope.

Beneath her fingers, Isamaru suddenly rolled onto his belly

and growled. His lip curled up over his sharp white teeth, wrinkling the flesh on his massive square head.

"Isamaru," she said sharply. "Be quiet."

The dog continued to stare at the corner of the room, growling ominously.

"There's nothing there, old friend." Michiko rose from her chair and took a step toward the corner. "See? It's just—"

Isamaru interrupted her with a single loud, throaty bark. He also rose to his feet, but he kept his body close to the ground as he crept forward, snarling and sniffing.

The daylight was diffused by both the clouds overhead and the fog that permeated Eiganjo, but the light was still strong enough to cast shadows across Michiko's cell. The corner of the room was half-obscured under a dark square created by the window frame and the curtains.

"Easy there, blockhead," came a rich, smooth voice. Michiko saw no one, though she was staring directly at the source of the sound. The voice sounded familiar in its cadence and tone and its choice of words. The princess's heart began to beat faster.

Toshi Umezawa emerged from the shadows, his face wreathed in a triumphant grin.

"Hello, Princess. I got your message."

Isamaru let out a long series of barks that ran together like one long word. Michiko took hold of the huge dog's collar to keep him from lunging. He could have easily pulled her along with him, but he had been trained to respect the hand that guided him.

Toshi had retreated back into the shadow, leaving the corner apparently empty.

"Someone's sure to come investigate that," the ochimusha's

voice said. Sure enough, footsteps were approaching her room as the guards came down the hallway.

"Not to say it doesn't come to you naturally," Toshi whispered, "but act innocent."

Michiko turned to face the window, her hand still on Isamaru's collar. She waited as the sentries unbarred and unlocked the door.

One of her father's stewards pushed the door open and stepped inside. Two dour samurai stood respectfully in the hall, waiting.

The steward bowed. "Is everything all right, Princess?"

"Of course. Isamaru is feeling playful." She stroked the big dog's muzzle. "He's growing tired of sitting still all day."

The steward nodded. "Would you like us to take him back to the kennels?"

Michiko paused. "Yes," she said. "Perhaps a change of scenery will do him good."

The steward whistled, and Michiko released the dog's collar. Isamaru took one last glance at the shadows in the corner, licked the princess's hand, then bounded past the steward into the hall.

"Excuse the intrusion, Princess." The steward bowed again as he backed from the room.

"Not at all." Michiko listened to the key turning in the lock and then to the bar being replaced. She began counting to herself as soon as the sentries' footsteps had faded away.

She reached sixty before Toshi cautiously emerged from the shadows once more.

"Well done." He grinned.

Michiko was amazed all over again. "How did . . . where did you—"

"Hey, hey. You wanted a rescue, right?"

Dumbly, the princess nodded.

"Well, I'm here to rescue you." Toshi scanned the inside of the cell. "Eventually. Will you be safe here for another few hours?"

"I think so."

"Good. This trip was a test, to see if I could get in. Now that I know I can, I need to square a few more things away before I take you out of here. Oh, and there is the matter of payment."

"Payment?"

Toshi nodded. "People like you have jobs that need doing. People like me take care of them for you. Nobody does it for free, Princess."

Michiko scowled. She quickly scanned the room, then remembered the small blue jewel she wore on her finger. Disdainfully, she pulled the ring off and offered it to Toshi.

"Will this cover your expenses?"

Toshi leaned farther into the room, peering at the jewel. Before Michiko could say anything else, he had snatched it from her fingers and tucked it away inside his shirt.

"Doubly so. I apologize, Princess, but it's best to keep things as strictly professional as possible."

Michiko stared at him icily. "Of course."

"I'll be back before sundown. Be ready."

"But where are you—"

"No time," Toshi said again. His eyes twinkled. "Just sit tight and you'll be free before you know it."

Toshi receded back into the pale shadow until he'd vanished from sight.

Confused and angry, Michiko turned back toward the window and drew a piece of paper from the pile on her writing desk. She carefully folded the sheet, performing the first few steps that would transform it from a flat square into a three-dimensional bird. She made a mistake on the fifth fold.

She wished she could trust Toshi more. She wished she hadn't given him the ring but had held it as a deposit against his return. Especially since now that she had paid, she couldn't imagine what was more important than getting her out of the tower.

Sighing, Michiko unfolded the piece of paper and started again.

* * * * *

Toshi appeared just outside Hidetsugu's wall of heads on sticks, emerging from a darkened cleft in the rocks. Using the Shadow Gate's power was taxing, but he could already feel his body adjusting to it. He hoped it would be like long-distance running: the more he did it, the less exhausting it was.

Toshi crept along the edges of the path, carefully watching for any signs of movement ahead. He had attempted to sneak into Shinka only once before, when he was part of Uramon's reckoners. The plan had been to take the ogre unawares and poison him to clear the way for a new black market trade route through the Sokenzan. Hidetsugu had sent Uramon's first delegation back partially devoured and without their heads, so the Boss had been eager to make an example of him.

Things had not gone as planned. Toshi was the only survivor. He did not relish the thought of trespassing in Hidetsugu's hut once again.

At least this time he was alone. If the ogre stayed true to his nature, he had already gathered his yamabushi dogs and headed into the Jukai Forest. Toshi crept along until he could see the ogre's hut. Smoke still rose from the entrance, but it was not billowing as it had when he brought Marrow and Kiku here.

He paused, summoning up a mental image of the Myojin of Night's Reach. He closed his eyes, concentrated, and faded from sight. Toshi made his slow, meticulous way down the ramp.

He needn't have bothered with the disappearing act. There was no fire, no chanting, and no sign of Hidetsugu or his captive warrior mages. Toshi willed himself solid again and quickly crossed the dank cavern floor.

His memory was good, and the scent of choking smoke grew thicker as he approached his goal. The ill-fated wizard Choryu still hung from the wall, even more wretched and diminished than Toshi had seen him earlier. The ochimusha stepped to the pinned figure and looked up.

"I don't know if you deserve this," Toshi said.

Blind, barely conscious, Choryu moaned.

Toshi scowled. "If it were up to me, I'd leave you here. I liked Kobo. But in the grand scheme of things, wizard, you just aren't that important."

He latched on to a bump in the cavern wall and hauled himself up on it. He dug his toes into a crack in the rock then plunged his free hand into Choryu's chest.

The wizard thrashed and howled incoherently. Toshi felt the hot gem in his hand and he closed his fist around it. With one last look at Choryu's ruined face, Toshi tore the glowing stone free.

Choryu screamed anew. The wizard's dying sound was a wet, hissing wheeze. His body sagged from the thick spikes holding him in place.

Toshi waited a moment to make sure Choryu's breathing had

stopped, then the ochimusha crammed the dusty orange gem back into the dead body's torso.

Fresh back smoke poured from the hole in the corpse. Slowly, Choryu's body flaked away, breaking up into a cloud of ashes, dust, and leathery shards. In a matter of moments, the wall was empty, and the orange gem was perched atop a sad pile of grit and debris on the alcove floor.

Toshi dropped from the wall and headed straight for the ramp that led to the surface. Hidetsugu would be furious when he returned, but Toshi saw two possible ways to escape the ogre's retribution.

In the first, he completed his tasks before Hidetsugu reached the academy. All went well, and he had enough power to discourage even an o-bakemono from trifling with him.

In the second, Hidetsugu reached the academy first and wiped out the students, the instructors, the soratami, and their patron kami. In the wake of such a victory, Hidetsugu would scarcely notice or care that he could no longer play with his favorite toy.

Any other outcome would probably result in bad blood between Toshi and Hidetsugu, and he decided not to entertain such thoughts. They would only bring him grief.

He didn't realize he was running until he was halfway up the ramp. He didn't stop until he was well clear of the ogre's hut, whereupon he disappeared into the shadows on its far side.

* * * * *

Lady Pearl-Ear had withdrawn from the main party to meditate and collect her thoughts. So far, the journey to Minamo had gone smoothly, albeit slowly. They had sent runners ahead to announce their arrival, and the kitsune rangers said they were less than two days from the edge of the waterfall.

She settled onto a pile of leaves under a huge tree and closed her eyes. Captivity and solitude in the tower had had one advantage that she hadn't realized: it precluded her brother from filling her ears with his endless chatter. He had been extra-animated since her return, and now she relished this chance to sit alone in silence.

"Pssst. Hey, Pearl-Ear."

Pearl-Ear kept her eyes closed, but her entire body tensed for action. She had heard no one approach.

"Who is there? Excuse me please, I was just taking a moment for myself."

"Take all the time you need. I'll be here when you're done. You were really hard to find. Where are we, anyway?"

Pearl-Ear kept her eyes closed, but tilted her head back. She could not sense the speaker by sound or aura-smell, but she was starting to recognize the voice.

"Toshi," she said. She opened her eyes. "You are not welcome here, murderer. Begone before I summon the Tail brothers."

There was no sign of the kanji mage except for his dry, mocking chuckle. His voice moved around her so that she could not pinpoint his location.

"Is that a threat? Because you know I walked right out from under them last time."

"True, but I'm sure they'd appreciate another opportunity, all the same." Pearl-Ear made as if to rise.

"If I leave," Toshi said, "how will you know when to expect Michiko?"

Pearl-Ear's eyes grew fierce. "You stay away from her, ochi-musha."

"Can't. She's hired me to spring her from the tower. I even got paid in advance."

"You must not," Pearl-Ear snapped savagely. "The daimyo will—"

"I didn't ask the daimyo," Toshi said. "I asked her, and she wanted out, so I'm going to get her out. After that, whether I bring her here or somewhere else is totally up to you."

Pearl-Ear calmed herself. "What do you want?"

"Well, Michiko-hime is my employer, so I want what she wants."

"And that is?"

"She wants to be free and safe. I think she still wants to go to the academy for answers about what her father did on the night she was born, but I can tell you truly: the academy is not going to be a safe place for anyone. Maybe not ever again. If you can promise to keep away from the school, I'll bring her to you tonight."

"And if I will not bargain with you?"

"I will stash her in the nastiest rat's nest I can find. You and your friends can search Numai until you wither and die, but you'll never see her again."

Pearl-Ear paused. Was there any reason to tell him the truth, especially as it involved the princess? There were a host of good reasons not to, chief among them his habit of taking her on jaunts halfway across Kamigawa.

"If you bring Michiko to me," she said, "I will keep her safe. I can offer you no more."

Toshi also waited before responding. "I can never tell when

you foxes are lying," he said. "You should take that as a compliment."

"Strangely, I do not, but thank you just the same."

"Fair enough." Toshi shimmered into view a short distance away, close enough to be heard but far enough to avoid Pearl-Ear if she lunged.

"I do not trust you, Toshi. I cannot, no matter how much I may want to. I would do almost anything to free Michiko, but I will never agree to place her in your hands."

Toshi tilted his head. "Why not? I took good care of her last time I kidnapped her."

Pearl-Ear growled ominously. "You'd do well not to speak of that episode. You have yet to answer for Choryu."

"Choryu's dead," Toshi said coldly, "and I will answer for it proudly. He murdered one of the hyozan, and the hyozan saw to him." He placed his hands on his hips and stared boldly into Pearl-Ear's face. "You are a good judge of character, Lady. I can tell that. Look me in the eye and judge me now: Yes, we made Choryu suffer, but I swear that I treated him mercifully in the end."

Pearl-Ear held Toshi's eyes. He was crafty, dishonest, and manipulative, but she was from a society of tricksters. He was telling her the truth. "Very well," she said. "I do not recognize the authority of your oath or your murderous band. Few in this world are wise enough to dispense justice.

"Nonetheless, I accept that you believe Choryu did you wrong and that you reacted according to the rules of your harsh and brutal world." She bowed briefly. "I accept only that. Now. What must I do for you to bring Michiko here?"

Toshi winked. "Meet us here, tonight, by this tree, but

be advised, Lady. Once I give her to you, she becomes your responsibility."

"She has always been that," Pearl-Ear said. "Why are you doing this, ochimusha? I see no profit in this for you."

Toshi smiled. "Recently, I got religion."

Pearl-Ear's face was impassive. She crossed her arms.

Toshi's expression fell. "Why is it so hard for everyone to believe that?"

Pearl-Ear shrugged. "Perhaps you do not have a honest face. In fact, you look unwell. Are you even able to rescue Michiko?" Indeed, the ochimusha seemed pale and his breathing hitched whenever he drew anything more than a shallow breath.

"I have been traveling long distances today. It is a wearying experience. Don't worry. If I can't make it here, I'll take her somewhere safe. You have my word."

Pearl-Ear did not reply but stared skeptically as Toshi faded from view.

She said a silent prayer to the kami of the woods. She feared the outlaw's word meant only what he said it did and nothing more.

Please, she thought. This time, let that be enough.

* * * * *

Toshi stepped out onto the ridge overlooking the border between the Sokenzan Mountains and Towabara. The stabbing pain in his chest and the fog in his brain grew worse with each jaunt, but he was nearly done. He just needed to make sure Hidetsugu had done as he'd been asked before he could return to the tower.

Despite the stress on his body, Toshi was growing accustomed to the power of the Shadow Gate, choosing his destinations and arriving within ten or twenty yards of his target. It helped if he were moving toward someone he knew or to a place he'd been before. With a little practice, he felt that soon he could go anywhere in Kamigawa.

A cold wind blew up from the valley floor below. Toshi leaned over the edge of the ridge, watching the small figures scurrying below.

A woman in white floated eerily between three of the daimyo's soldiers. One was lying supine on the rocky ground, his eyes open and vacant to the sky. Another was curled into a tight, shivering ball with his hands clapped hard over his ears. The third was being caressed by the woman, her hand tenderly stroking his cheek.

The wind changed, and the woman's hair blew back from her face. The third soldier dropped stiffly to the ground, and she floated toward the second, who still lay shuddering and helpless.

Toshi watched the thing that looked like Princess Michiko lay hands on the final soldier. The man stiffened under her touch, and his trembling ceased.

Toshi shook his head. As he'd feared, she was too powerful. He hadn't been able to control the aspect of shadow that drew on her essence, and it had consumed all of Uramon's manor. Left unchecked, the yuki-onna herself would likewise engulf the entire border.

Toshi stepped back from the edge of the rock before the figure of Michiko could glance up and spot him. As he melted back into the shadows, he vowed to do something about the snow woman. Eventually, she would evolve from something that endangered his enemies to something that endangered everyone. Eventually he'd have to take steps to prevent that from happening.

Toshi nodded to himself as he soared through the void of shadows. Eventually.

* * * * *

Michiko sat once more at her writing desk. She had folded origami, she had paced, she had done everything she could think of to busy her mind and relieve the stress of waiting. Now she sat and stared, looking out the window as she watched the corner with her peripheral vision.

She wished she had not sent Isamaru back to the kennels. The more she thought on it, the more she realized it would be good to have a loyal dog at her side if she were to travel with Toshi.

Assuming the ochimusha ever came back. He was probably in a dreary little tavern in Numai, spending the money he'd gotten in exchange for her ring.

"Pssst. Princess. Ready to go?"

Michiko remained calm and continued to look out the window. She nodded, however, an almost imperceptible bob of the head.

Toshi appeared like a ghost, stepping from the shadowed corner. The room had grown much darker in the fading sunlight, but she could see his features clearly as he came out of the gloom.

The ochimusha looked haggard, as if he had seen and done too much. His eyes were dim, but he still wore his rakish smile. He extended his arm.

"Take my hand, Princess. I've not taken fellow travelers with me often enough to be overconfident."

She wrapped her fingers around his. His hand was very cold. "I would settle for merely confident. How many times *have* you done this?"

"None," he admitted cheerfully. "None times."

"I wish to go to Minamo academy," she said. "Can you take me there?"

"No, Princess. It is protected by spells more powerful than mine."

Michiko's eyes narrowed. "The spells that protect this tower are the most powerful in all Kamigawa, yet you had no trouble coming here."

"Nonetheless." Toshi's smile grew strained. "I can't take you there. I have something better in mind."

Michiko dropped Toshi's hand. "I am having second thoughts, ochimusha. The last time I went with you, you intended to ransom me."

"Your hands were bound then," Toshi said, "and we hadn't come to an arrangement." The blue ring appeared in his hands as if conjured directly from his pocket. "This buys my loyalty until the job is done. Why else did you think I insisted on payment? It's for your peace of mind as much as my purse."

Michiko stared hard at Toshi. Slowly, she extended her hand and allowed him to grasp it firmly.

"If I may," he said. Gently, he spread her palm and fingers wide and pressed them into the center of his breastbone. She felt something squirming like a small snake under her touch.

"Good," he said. "Now, relax, and close your eyes. In a moment, you'll be among friends."

Michiko smiled coldly. "So I am not now?"

Toshi cocked his head. "You're not my friend, you're my employer. It's best to keep things—"

"Strictly business," she finished. She placed her other hand on Toshi's chest. "Please. I want to get away from here."

"Close your eyes," Toshi said again.

Michiko closed her eyes. She felt the strangest sensation, as if her body had melted and left only her mind. She felt a tug on her phantom arms and was plunged into an endless sea of black.

PART TWO

MOONRISE
OVER THE FALLS

A white rain descends
Drops of light from darkened skies
Illuminate the void

General Takeno stood outside the door to the daimyo's private sanctuary deep in the center of the building. Though there were sentries and soldiers aplenty on each level of the tower, no guards were posted outside this final threshold. Takeno and the daimyo's other top advisors would have preferred to have warriors standing by at all times, but Konda refused.

"Not even the kami would dare attack me here," he once said, and so far he'd been proven correct.

Takeno's breathing was labored. He was no longer a young man, and the trip from ground level to the very top of the daimyo's tower was difficult. His legs had weakened, and his joints had stiffened over the years, but he could still ride and fire a bow better than anyone in Konda's army. Sometimes he toyed with the idea of riding to the top of the tower to spare his aging knees—certainly the stairs could accommodate his mount.

The general had served Daimyo Konda for almost thirty years. From his humble beginnings as a cavalry officer over a single unit, he had risen to supreme command of the daimyo's entire mounted army. He had fought at Konda's behest and at the daimyo's side, and together they had achieved great things.

Takeno would gladly lay down his life for his lord and for Eiganjo, knowing full well that every soldier in his command would do the same.

Along with his fatigue, it was Takeno's devotion to Konda that caused him to hesitate on the verge of the daimyo's private rooms. He hated to bring his lord bad news from the frontier, especially when the situation here was so desperate. But the general had always presented Konda with the most accurate and up to date assessment of their campaigns, no matter how sobering. They had suffered reversals before and prevailed. He shook off his weariness and his doubts and put his trust once more in Daimyo Konda.

"My lord," Takeno spoke as he climbed the short staircase. He did not expect an answer, but he did want to alert Konda to his presence. The daimyo was becoming more distant than ever, and the more time he spent communing with his prize, the less aware he seemed of the world outside.

Takeno reached the doorway at the top of the stairs. He steeled himself, opened the door, and called out again.

"My lord. I bring news from the bandit frontier."

The old soldier could see Konda through the open door. He was at the far end of the room, kneeling before a thick pedestal with his back to Takeno. A rough stone disk hovered above the pedestal, throwing off a harsh white glare and steaming as if it had just been drawn from a boiling pot. Konda spent hours each day bathing in that glare, breathing in that steam. When he laid hands on the disk, the glow spread to him and surrounded his body, as if the disk and the ruler were awash with the same energy.

Takeno knew the disk's face bore the carved outline of a fetal

---

dragon, but he did not look at it. Doing so always made him shudder, which never failed to annoy Konda. Takeno had been present on the night the daimyo created the thing with a ritual that required the assistance of a mysterious soratami mage and Minamo's highest-ranking wizard. Takeno would do anything for his master, but he prayed that Konda would never ask him to revisit that terrible night.

The general still believed Konda when the daimyo declared the act would lead to the ultimate salvation of all Kamigawa. Takeno also prayed nightly for that salvation to come, and quickly, before there was nothing left of the daimyo's kingdom to save.

"Daimyo Konda," he said loudly. Though he was old and out of breath, his voice still carried enough force to command the attention of a thousand men assembled for battle.

Konda lifted his head. He did not turn to face the general but said, "Ahh, Takeno. I have only to think about you, and here you are. Yosei is an awesome sight, is he not?"

"He is, my lord. The people sing the Morning Star's praises daily, and yours. There have been almost no deaths from kami attacks since you summoned him."

"Excellent. The wizards of Minamo have already followed my advice and raised their own dragon: Keiga the Tide Star, who stands as Yosei's brother in the company of spirit dragons. It is part of my new campaign against the other kami—the myojin may be exalted, but they are no more formidable than the guardian dragons of Kamigawa itself."

Takeno nodded slowly. "An excellent stratagem, my lord."

"I must find a way to raise the others," Konda said, "the guardians of Jukai and Sokenzan. Perhaps even the dark spirit dragon of Takenuma could be compelled to join our cause."

The daimyo rose, trailing his hand along the stone disk as he stood, then turned to face Takeno. The General bowed, using his obeisance as a pretext to avoid looking into Konda's eyes.

Takeno did not understand the link between Konda and the stone disk, nor did he care to, but it was clear that the ritual that created the prize had also bestowed semi-divine powers upon the ruler. Ever since the night Michiko was born and the prize was taken from the kakuriyo, Konda's eyes had been stricken with that eerie drift, vacillating from side to side within his sockets. He had also shown flashes of incredible strength and demonstrated knowledge of events on the far side of the world.

In his most private thoughts, Takeno resented the stone disk. To him and the rest of the army, Konda had been godlike without the benefit of magic and divine vision. The force of the daimyo's personality and the skill of his retainers was more than enough to unite a nation—commandeering the spirits to cement that union was unnecessary at best and vulgar at worst.

Now Konda approached him, still glittering with the stone disk's power. His eyes bounced slowly back and forth as he strode up to Takeno.

"Why have you come, General? Did I summon you?"

Takeno bowed again. "No, my lord. I have come to report disturbing dispatches from the border guards along the Sokenzan range."

"Ah. Do so."

"My lord, the commander of the unit stationed there reports that Godo has employed a powerful new spell that appears to either increase the cold or negate our army's efforts to keep warm. We have lost nearly one-tenth of our forces to the

weather, which is far worse than normal for that region. The
bandits are visible, but they are not taking any aggressive action.
They are merely watching and waiting while our troops freeze
to death."

Konda gestured impatiently. "Send them more cold-weather
gear," he said.

"There are . . . more disturbing aspects to the dispatch, my
lord. Most of the fallen soldiers inexplicably abandoned their
posts before they froze. Sentries go missing, only to turn up dead
far from where they were assigned. Patrols equipped for freezing
weather die fully dressed, their bodies scattered a short distance
from one another."

Konda leveled his strange eyes at Takeno. "This sounds like
a discipline problem. Have they forgotten the basics of winter
warfare? Tell them to burn more campfires and stay closer to
them."

"My lord," Takeno said. "There are also unconfirmed reports
. . . rumors . . . that your daughter has been seen along the
border. The sight of her is enough to send the bravest and most
disciplined soldier into harm's way. Meanwhile, the casualties
continue to mount, no matter what steps are taken, and morale
is declining rapidly."

Konda growled, his voice harsh and urgent. "My daughter,"
he said, "is in the tower, not three floors below where we stand.
Am I such a joke among my own troops that they believe I would
lose track of my daughter twice in the same year?"

"Certainly not, my lord. The commander fears that Godo is
using a look-alike to lure your loyal retainers into ambush, stun-
ning them, and leaving them to freeze in the cold."

"My daughter wandered off once. She would not dishonor me

so a second time. And I will not be goaded by the likes of that sanzoku dog."

"My lord," Takeno said. He swallowed hard. "This morning the sentries posted outside your daughter's room reported that it is empty. They did not see her leave. While they searched for hours, it seems Princess Michiko is no longer in the tower."

Konda's face grew tight, though his eyes continued to drift. "How is this possible?"

"I cannot say, my lord. She must have had outside help."

"This look-alike on the Sokenzan border," he said. "Could this be Michiko herself?"

"No, my lord. The timing is wrong—the look-alike appeared while the princess was still inside the tower."

"This is outrageous. This is unacceptable."

Takeno bowed.

"Find my daughter," the daimyo growled. "Find her and bring her before me. Send riders into Numai, the Araba, and into the depths of hell itself. This will not stand!"

"It shall be done, my lord."

Konda composed himself. "The bandit chief seeks to provoke me. Well, he has done so. Let him now suffer the consequences."

"My lord, if I may—"

"Concentrate all available companies on the Sokenzan border. Spread them along its length."

"Please, my lord—"

Konda was lost in his own mind. "Godo obviously wants us to focus on that one area, but we will not be fooled. Most likely he plans to penetrate the border somewhere else and sneak a large force of his sanzoku into our territory." The daimyo looked up. "Make sure the new companies are mobile and ready to respond quickly. They should patrol the entire border regularly, converging on any group of bandits numbering more than a dozen."

"As you wish, my lord, but we do not have enough reserves to cover the entire border."

Konda, who had started to turn back to his prize, stopped. He narrowed one strange eye at Takeno.

"Explain."

"The kami attacks on Eiganjo led us to pull most of our army off regular duty and station them here. There are enough border troops to monitor the bandits but not to engage them. If we spread them any thinner, they will be vulnerable. If Godo is able to exploit this, we could lose the entire force."

Konda raised a clenched fist. "I will send Yosei to the mountains, where he can destroy Godo and his bandit rabble once and for all."

Takeno lowered his head. "As you wish, my lord. Who, then, will protect Eiganjo from the kami?"

"We will, old friend. We will. You have seen how quickly the dragon moves, how fiercely he fights. Surely the armies of Eiganjo can protect one city for a few days. That is all the time the Morning Star will need."

Takeno kept his head bowed. "As you wish, Daimyo Konda."

He heard the daimyo straighten up. "You are not convinced?"

"I am cautious, my lord. We are far from full strength and have been so for months. A new campaign, among all the other crises the army is facing, would put a huge stress on a system that is already taxed to the breaking point."

Konda placed a hand on Takeno's shoulder. "You do not comprehend the dragon's power, General. That is why you hesitate. Come. I will show you the full scope of Yosei in combat."

The daimyo spun Takeno around and draped his arm across the general's shoulders. He steered Takeno over to the door, tilting his head for one last glance at the prize on its pedestal. Marching the general down the short staircase, Konda extolled the dragon's virtues and waving excitedly as they went. As they passed the daimyo's personal guard, all twelve retainers fell in step, keeping a respectful distance behind.

"Yosei is blinding," Konda said. "His speed, his power, the righteous glow that surrounds him. He could travel to the mountains and back in a single day. I doubt it will take him longer than that to destroy Godo's horde down to the last bandit. With your finest horsemen outside the gates, my moths in the air, and our best-trained troops inside to protect the populace, our losses will be minimal. Those of our enemy will be total. You will see, Takeno. In this new era I am ushering in, wars will be decided not by force of arms but by the will of a single ruler. I have planted the seeds for a kingdom based on spiritual power as well as martial strength. Yosei is but the first bloom I have harvested."

As they shuffled from the center of the tower to its outer edge, sentries, soldiers, and servants all stepped aside. The civilians bowed and sang Konda's praises, the retainers stood rigid and saluted.

Takeno's head swam, both from shortness of breath and from Konda's overwhelming presence. It was like standing near an open furnace whose heat and vapors sapped the strength from mind and body alike.

At last, they reached the exterior wall and the grand doorway that led outside. Except for the observation level at the very top of the tower, this balcony offered the clearest view of southern Towabara. If not for the haze and the yellow clouds, Takeno could have seen the tips of the Sokenzan.

"Behold, Konda said. "The full majesty of—"

The daimyo never finished his thought. Instead, his hand tightened on Takeno's shoulder as they both stared at the spectacle just beyond the edge of the balcony.

Yosei, the Morning Star, guardian dragon spirit of the realm, was little more than a blur as he circled the tower. His body seemed to be a constant, uninterrupted ring as he went round and round like a dog chasing its tail. Takeno had to concentrate to spot the dragon's head, which overlapped the end of his streamlined body as he whirled around. Nearby, dozens of riders steered their battle moths clear of the frenzied guardian's path.

The haze was thinner today than it had been, allowing Takeno and Konda to see much more of the horizon. In fact, there was a large circular hole in the center of the cloud cover, the clear eye in a swirling storm of yellow fog.

Yosei continued to race around them. Takeno heard the rising screech of the dragon's increasingly panicked cry. He craned his head and peered into the clear, calm center of the sky.

"My lord," he said, pointing. "Do you see that?"

Konda did not answer, but he dropped his arm from Takeno's shoulder and shuffled to the stone railing at the end of the balcony. His vacillating eyes were fixed on the same spot Takeno had pointed out.

In the far-off sky, a flame sparked to life in the calm center of the storm. A similar spark flared nearby, mirroring the first, but at this distance it was impossible to gauge how large the flames were or how far apart.

The twin fireballs moved as one, orienting on Konda's tower like a great pair of eyes. A second matching pair opened behind the first, then a third. Each pair moved together but independently from the others. All the flaming orbs fixed on Eiganjo then stopped, hovering ominously in the sky.

Takeno felt a rush of air flow past him as something unimaginably vast inhaled. Then, the old soldier dropped to his knees as an ear-splitting roar rolled up southern Towabara and slammed into the tower like a gale-force wind.

Blood dribbled from the general's ears. Beneath his feet, Konda's mighty tower shuddered, and for a delirious moment Takeno wondered if it too was frightened.

On the horizon the matching pairs of eyes began to move. Fog, smoke, or something unknown was coalescing around the huge flaming orbs. It appeared as if each set of eyes was housed within a great reptilian head that was still taking shape, each perched on top of a long and sinuous neck. Their progress was slow and ponderous, but they were definitely coming straight for Eiganjo.

Takeno climbed to his feet and went to Konda's side at the rail. The daimyo's eyes were steady and fixed on the monstrosity slowly inching its way toward them.

"My lord," Takeno gasped. "What is happening?"

Konda did not seem frightened but resolute. He gripped the balcony railing before slamming his closed fist into his open palm.

"It has come at last," Konda whispered. "As we were told it might."

Takeno forgot himself and tugged on the daimyo's sleeve. "Forgive me, my lord, but I am at a loss. What has come? Who warned us?"

"The Great Spirit Beast," Konda said. Takeno noticed his eyes begin drifting anew. "O-Kagachi, the Great Old Serpent. The embodiment of the kakuriyo itself has come to claim The Taken One, that which now rightfully belongs to me."

Konda turned suddenly, tossing off Takeno's hand.

"Order all available troops to the Sokenzan border as we discussed. Yosei is needed here, to aid me in my struggle against O-Kagachi." Konda paused, musing. "I must also send word to Minamo. Keiga must also prepare for this battle."

The daimyo turned and clasped both hands on Takeno's shoulders. "When you have dispatched your riders, return to me. We must repair to my sanctuary to meditate, commune, and prepare for the great serpent's arrival. This will be a decisive battle, old friend, one that we must win."

Takeno struggled not to swoon. Before him, the daimyo's mad eyes swam back and forth. In the distance, a vast, three-headed titan was crawling across the sky.

"I am your servant, my lord." Takeno stepped back and saluted. "I will do as you command."

CHAPTER 14

Pearl-Ear waited under the waning moon, near the tree where she had seen and heard Toshi. Externally, she was a study in calm, but she could barely keep her hands from shaking as she sat.

She did not, in fact, expect the ochimusha to show up. Toshi was a cunning man and a careful one, so he had to be aware of the bad blood that existed between himself and the kitsune. On their last outing he had insulted them, kidnapped the princess, sent Choryu to an unknown fate, and escaped from their custody, all with a sneer and a sarcastic comment. Her brother was eager to lay hands on Toshi, and the Tail brothers were likely to run him through on sight.

Pearl-Ear had been able to keep secret her meeting with Toshi, at least from Sharp-Ear and the Tails. Instead, she had confided in Captain Silver-Foot and Riko-ome from the academy. Silver-Foot had a low opinion of most humans and Riko, who had been on the outing that resulted in Toshi's capture of Michiko, bore the same grudges as the kitsune brothers. Both the student and the officer had cooler heads and a better understanding of duty than the others, however, and Pearl-Ear felt she had to trust them. The alternative would be to go to Toshi's meeting place alone.

Pearl-Ear shifted slightly under her tree. She could sense Riko, concealed among the cedar leaves overhead. She could not locate Silver-Foot, though she knew he and at least three of his rangers were positioned with a clear view of the area. Pearl-Ear was hopeful they would have a reasonable chance of catching Toshi or the princess, assuming they ever showed up.

Pale moonlight illuminated the trees, casting soft shadows along the ground. Pearl-Ear tilted her muzzle down. Her people were extremely sensitive to the natural order of things, and something decidedly unnatural was happening in the darkness. Though the night was cold and still, she sensed a motion from within the shadows on the ground.

Pearl-Ear leaned closer. No, not on the ground. For some reason, these dark shapes seemed to descend into the ground, plunging to depths she would never be able to fathom. Was this how Toshi could come and go so quickly?

All Pearl-Ear's questions, fears, and concerns vanished when the crown of a shiny, black-haired head broke through the cedar shadow. "Michiko-hime," she said, anxiety robbing her words of their force.

The princess rose from the black plane, rising like steam without apparent effort. She seemed fine, healthy and strong, if a little pale. Her eyes were closed, and she appeared to be in a deep sleep as she sprouted from the ground like a fast-growing weed.

Pearl-Ear stood in case Silver-Foot and his rangers could not see Michiko's arrival. She wanted armed warriors by her side when Toshi emerged and demanded payment.

Meanwhile, Michiko's tall, lithe form completed its vertical journey. Her toes still lay beneath the surface of the shadow, and her eyes were still shut, but she was whole and complete and as beautiful as ever. Pearl-Ear restrained herself from gathering her former student in her arms.

"Open your eyes," Toshi's voice said, "and step forward, princess."

Michiko's eyelids fluttered. She wavered on the surface of her shadowy perch, but as her eyes cleared she saw Pearl-Ear waiting with open arms.

"Sensei!" she cried. She stepped forward, dragging her foot through the shadow as if it were no more than a shallow puddle and placed her sandal on solid ground.

Pearl-Ear rushed forward, embracing the much larger princess with all her might, pulling her away from the dim pool that had spawned her. For a moment the fox-woman was able to forget kami, the daimyo's ire, and her own journey on behalf of her people. She had been reunited with Michiko at last, and she would let nothing spoil this perfect moment.

She stepped back and clamped onto Michiko's upper arms, staring into the princess's face.

"Are you all right?" Pearl-Ear said. "Is there anyone with you?"

"I am here, Lady Pearl-Ear." Toshi's voice echoed from within the shadow on the ground. "But I daresay if I show my face, someone will put an arrow through it."

Pearl-Ear did not look up, where Riko sat with her bow at the ready. The student wizard was likely to shoot Toshi just to clear the way for her own reunion with Michiko.

"You have nothing to fear," Pearl-Ear said, "so long as you have no surprises planned."

Pearl-Ear heard a whisper of steel just before the razored edge of a blade pressed tight against her throat.

"None, Lady." Toshi had appeared directly behind her, crouching between Pearl-Ear and the cedar tree. "And you? Kitsune are well-known for playing tricks. What lurks in yonder woods?"

Pearl-Ear held perfectly still. "Riko-ome is in the tree above, ochimusha. There are also rangers about. I thought it prudent to have someone to guard me while I waited."

"Toshi," Michiko said sternly. "Release Lady Pearl-Ear."

"In a moment, Princess. He leaned close to Pearl-Ear's ear and said, "I'm glad to see you're keeping your wits about you, Lady. I have done what I said I would do. The princess is now in your care."

The blade vanished. Pearl-Ear whirled around and locked her furious gaze on Toshi.

The ochimusha looked even less healthy than he had before. His skin was pale and drawn, his eyes were cloudy, and he seemed to suffer with each new breath. Pearl-Ear fought off a reflexive wave of sympathy—no matter how taxing the journey had been, Toshi was still too unpredictable to be considered a friend.

"Remember what we talked about," he said. He looked at the thin crescent moon overhead. In the pale moonlight, she could see him fading away like a ghost. "Take her somewhere safe."

The ochimusha was gone.

Riko slid down the tree trunk with her bow and an arrow in the same hand. When her feet touched the soil, she cast her weapons aside and rushed to Michiko, her eyes wild and wet.

As the two girls embraced, Pearl-Ear waved for Silver-Foot.

In seconds, he and the three kitsune rangers had materialized out of the darkness.

"Welcome to the Jukai, princess." Silver-Foot bowed, and the rangers followed his example. Michiko was still locked in Riko's arms, and neither girl noticed the warriors' respectful gesture.

The kitsune captain turned to Pearl-Ear. "So that was your kanji mage? Whatever he's using to appear and disappear like that will kill him if he's not careful."

"I expect he is aware of that," Pearl-Ear said. "He tends to be exceedingly careful."

"As do I," Silver-Foot said. "With your permission, I will lead you and your charges back to the camp site."

"By all means." Pearl-Ear stepped forward and placed a hand on each girl's shoulder.

"Come," she said. "There are safer places for a reunion, and I know several who will be almost delighted as we are to see you again, Princess."

Michiko laughed, and Riko squeezed her hand.

"Almost," the wizard said.

* * * * *

Toshi followed from a short distance as the kitsune led Michiko through the woods.

He was glad to see that the kitsune's heightened senses still could not detect his phantom form. He was getting better at moving around in this state. He would never be able to match a fox warrior at a full run, but he could keep pace as they hiked through the dark, close enough to hear what they were saying all the way back to their campsite.

Toshi again marveled at the size of the party—dozens of kit-sune warriors and a handful of Konda's cavalry. He wasn't sure what they were doing this deep in the Jukai, but he doubted it concerned him much. They looked like the remnants of a larger force, perhaps one that had been battling rogue kami and lost.

Lady Pearl-Ear and Riko led the princess to a large lean-to on the edge of the camp. Toshi recognized Sharp-Ear and the three kitsune warriors he had met before. He had never bothered to learn their names.

Toshi drifted to the very edge of the lean-to. He was glaring at Pearl-Ear as his mind worked. The last time this group had assembled, it had been to take Michiko into orochi country on some sort of pilgrimage. The snakes and the forest monks had attacked them without provocation and taken them all captive.

They wouldn't be stupid enough to try again, even with a bigger force behind them. This new party had a far more regimented feel to it, with the soldiers marching in ranks and ceremonial sashes on some of the foxes. The snakefolk lived wild and had no embassy, no spokesman. What could this official-looking delegation do in the woods except pass through?

Toshi watched as the kitsune brothers walked straight up him and scanned the exterior of the lean-to. One of them passed right through Toshi, unaware of the ochimusha's presence.

"We are alone," the warrior said.

"Thank you, Dawn-Tail. Michiko, we have very little time, so pay attention. We shall arrive on the shores in two days. We are expected, but you are a surprise. I think you should stay out of sight."

Toshi nodded to himself. He felt the familiar dread of being forced in the direction he least wanted to go.

"I disagree, sensei. If the delegation is from both Eiganjo and the kitsune nation—"

"You do not represent Eiganjo," Pearl-Ear said quietly, "and Headmaster Hisoka is a close friend and ally to your father. He will be obliged to return you to the tower or at least to report that you have come to him."

Toshi watched Pearl-Ear closely, trying to detect any sign of her inner thoughts. It was no use. Her face was too alien and her body language too elegant. She had lied right to his face and he had missed it. They were taking Michiko to the academy.

"How am I to avoid being seen?" the princess flared. "Am I to travel in someone's pack?"

"Don't be flip. We will disguise you in some of my robes. You will be my attendant."

"I am twice as tall as you, sensei."

"Then we will stitch two of my robes together. This is not open for debate, Princess. You are a fugitive, and you must not be seen. Our mission is too important."

The Princess gave a dismissive cough. "What is this mission?"

Toshi crept forward a few inches, listening carefully.

Pearl-Ear sighed. "Riko believes the school is hiding something. The masters lately have received frequent visits from the soratami above the falls. They are agitated, and became more so when . . ."

Riko stepped forward. "When I told them Choryu had died. They called me into Hisoka's offices and had me tell them the entire story . . . how we smuggled you out of the tower, how we wound up among the orochi. I explained how the ochimusha's friend was killed and how he accused Choryu of the murder. How he killed him for it. I asked if the ochimusha was right, because the evidence did support his claims.

"They didn't answer. They thanked me for my report and told me not to mention the subject to anyone. I was given duties that kept me away from my fellow students. That night, three soratami came down from their cloud city, three more the next morning. Since then, there have been daily visits.

"The headmaster is a good man, but I believe he and some of the other masters are working for the soratami, whom they revere as semi-divine. We all do. We are taught that they are exalted, far closer to the perfect balance of mind, body, and spirit than we humans."

Pearl-Ear spoke up. "Riko thinks this reverence has blinded the headmaster to the dangers we all face. He is pursuing the soratami agenda, working toward their goals. They do not see the Kami War as the rest of us see it."

"How can you say that?" Michiko said. "All Kamigawa has suffered during the war."

"The soratami have not been subjected to the same degree of attacks we have here on the ground. Their city floats above it all."

"That's not true," Riko said. "The academy is one of the busiest fronts in the war. I am part of an entire generation of students who trained for combat as well as academics. Minamo has contributed greatly to the defense of the utsushiyo."

"Of course they have," Pearl-Ear said, "but no one has ever seen their city in the clouds. It could be as devastated as the rest of Kamigawa, or it could be pristine and untouched. We cannot say."

"Nor can we say what the soratami intend without investigating further," Riko said. "I think it's clear they are influencing the headmaster, forcing him to do what they want. He seems frightened and awed every time they come. I know that if he had an ally . . . an ally like the kitsune . . . he could find the strength to resist them."

"If he had a confidant," Pearl-Ear added, "he might also reveal some of his most troublesome secrets."

The conversation continued, but Toshi slipped away into the woods. They were all fools, doomed fools. He had never heard Hisoka's name before tonight, but he'd bet his right arm that the headmaster would not welcome their offer of support anymore than he would answer their questions. If anything, the little toad would politely ask them to wait while he ran to the soratami for guidance.

You could never count on professors and politicians, who had raised bureaucracy and obfuscation to an art form. By the time they were through with the formal greetings and declarations of mutual support, Hidetsugu would have arrived and eaten half the academy.

Still, the idea of getting more information about the soratami appealed to him. They and their little crescent moon kami were definitely moving into Numai, and who knew what else they were up to? Perhaps Lady Pearl-Ear was right: The moonfolk saw the Kami War in their own terms, as nothing more than an opportunity.

Well clear of the campsite, Toshi paused. He was feeling good enough to travel again, as the dizziness and the pains in his chest had subsided. There was no shortage of shadows to employ, but he wasn't quite sure where to go.

He thought of Hidetsugu and his yamabushi. By now this lethal group would be tearing its way through the densest part of Jukai. Glancing up at the thin sliver of moon that remained, Toshi calculated he had three, maybe four days before the ogre reached Minamo.

Everyone was going to the school. The princess wanted answers, the kitsune wanted allies, and Hidetsugu wanted a row of heads on spikes that stretched all the way back to the mountains.

Toshi sighed to himself. Now would be the perfect time to continue his own journey, but circumstances were forcing him to delay that for just a little longer. There was too much at stake for him to let things spiral out of control now. He would have to stick around and keep an eye on the princess.

As he resigned himself to his decision, Toshi make sure not to look up at the crescent moon. He did not want to give Mochi the opportunity to take a good look at him, maybe see something that would warn the shifty blue kami.

Soon, the hyozan's best would bring their worst for the soratami and their patron spirit, and Toshi didn't want to ruin the surprise.

CHAPTER 15

The Kamitaki Falls was one of the largest and most spectacular natural features in all Kamigawa. It formed a horseshoe-shaped ridge that was over two thousand yards across at its widest point. The powerful Yumegawa River flowed over the jagged rocks and fell five hundred feet to the lake below. Spray and foam filled the air around the water's descent, and the surface of the lake was choppy and turbulent. Huge geysers blew columns of water all the way back up, almost to the edge of the falls, and billowing clouds of steam rolled across the shore.

Long ago, a group of scholars and learned wizards had come to this sacred spot, drawn by the magic inherent in the falls themselves. Through their combined efforts, they had been able to erect a massive walled structure that floated above the churning water and anchor it permanently to the center of the waterfall's sheer walls. They had also created a set of sturdy buildings that were supported by magical geysers—though they seemed precariously balanced, these structures were as solid as if their foundations were made of solid rock.

The wizards had gathered their students and begun to study the falls, the river, and all of the other arcane phenomena the local magic had created. Over the decades, more and more build-ings sprang up until the sheer drop was studded with dormitories, classrooms, and meditation chambers. The main building had always housed the senior staff, their offices, and the largest research library in all Kamigawa, but the other buildings were used for the students and the residents of the village that grew up around the school on the edge of the falls.

Taken together, the entire academy and its environs was a breathtaking sight. Everything glistened with the sheen of fresh, fast-moving water. The Minamo architects had maintained an organic feel to each individual building so that the entire campus looked as if it had sprouted naturally from the rock. From atop their geysers, gleaming blue steel spires stretched into the sky, and white-tiled roofs glittered under both sun and moon.

Bathed in the midday sun but obscured by thick clouds, the soratami capital floated high above both falls and academy. Otawara lurked among the clean white banks, offering only fleeting glimpses of its gleaming glass architecture.

Toshi scanned the faces of Michiko's party as they took in the splendor of Minamo. Riko's face was both relieved and anxious at the same time, but the others were serious and businesslike. Pearl-Ear and the littlest kitsune were looking for something, their heads darting back and forth as they gazed out over the water.

"Sharp-Ear," Pearl-Ear said. "It appears we are not going to be met. Would you engage us a ferryman, please?"

The little fox nodded and darted toward the water's edge. He would have no trouble—there were many boats on the water already, transporting people and cargo between the shore and the way station near the center of the lake. Most of the boats were large enough to carry the entire kitsune delegation with room to spare. Toshi could easily slip into some of that extra room and remain unnoticed all the way to the academy.

Sharp-Ear returned, having secured passage for the entire group. As the armed soldiers were marching down to the shore, a grand barge materialized out of the mist. Two formally dressed wizards stood at the prow, and the academy's insignia was emblazoned across the ship's hull.

Captains Silver-Foot and Nagao regrouped their soldiers into perfectly aligned ranks as Pearl-Ear, Sharp-Ear, and Riko stepped to the front. Pearl-Ear was attended by a tall girl who stayed concealed under her flowing white robes. Toshi smiled at Michiko's disguise. She was not only twice as tall as Pearl-Ear, she was twice as broad. Throw a sheet over him, and he'd make a more convincing kitsune attendant.

The three fox brothers stayed as close to the hidden figure as they dared without drawing more attention to her. Toshi didn't think they had to worry. Despite how much Michiko stood out, aristos like the academy masters rarely noticed servants. It was as if they'd been trained to see right through them. Pearl-Ear's choice of camouflage would serve the princess well.

They waited patiently as the wizards came down the gangplank and bowed before Pearl-Ear.

"Forgive us," the female wizard said. "I am Master Fuan of Minamo. This is Master Hon. We would have been here to greet you, but rough waves prevented us."

Pearl-Ear returned the bow. "Not at all. We are honored by your greeting. Will you take us to the headmaster now?"

"Of course. Hisoka is eager to hear your concerns."

"As we are eager to share them. Shall we go?"

"By all means. If you will follow me, I will lead you to the forward deck. Alas, there is not enough room for all your retainers."

Silver-Foot stepped forward. "Of course. If there is a cargo deck or a holding area large enough?"

The wizard relaxed. "There is." She indicated her partner, a pale fellow with brown hair and sleepy eyes. "Master Hon will take you to the assembly room on the middle deck. It is the largest room on the barge."

"Our thanks. I trust there is room enough for Lady Pearl-Ear's personal guard to accompany her." Silver-Foot jerked his head, and the three brothers stepped forward.

"Certainly," the wizard said, "though Headmaster Hisoka wishes me to assure you that you are quite safe here."

Pearl-Ear stepped in. "Captain Silver-Foot is merely being cautious. With so many kami attacks lately, we can never take our safety for granted."

Fuan nodded. "Things are in a terrible state, but we have made great progress here in containing the aggressive spirits. A short while ago, merchants would not brave the surface of the lake for fear of being capsized by hostile kami. Through hard work and powerful magic, we have restored the normal rhythm of our daily lives."

"That is quite comforting," Sharp-Ear said, "but may we continue on to the academy now? Safe or no, we have important matters to discuss with the headmaster."

"Of course," Fuan said. "We shall disembark directly."

The leaders of the kitsune delegation followed the wizards up onto the main deck. Toshi started up the gangplank while they were still on it. There seemed to be no limit to the gift given him by the Myojin of Night's Reach—not even the wizard's magic could pierce the veil that concealed him.

He boarded the boat and slipped quietly down to the lower decks. He had very little interest in a closer view of the wondrous falls, and he needed to find the galley or at least the food stores. He had been formless for the better part of two days and he desperately needed something to eat.

After all, he wanted to be at his best for his audience with the headmaster.

* * * * *

The city of Otawara was built on a cloud, its roots tightly woven into in the billowy white mass that hovered over Minamo. Like the academy below, Otawara had been built with ingenious magic that kept it aloft, but the soratami capital was even larger and grander than the school. The city itself was a collection of vast palaces with gleaming silver spires that glowed in the moonlight. It was said that no human had ever set foot inside the city, and the soratami who lived there would slaughter any who tried.

In the largest and highest tower, two of the city's most powerful residents were receiving a guest. They were both dressed in similar robes of deep, rich indigo with complex symbols embroidered into the hem with metallic silver thread. They were female, and they could have been sisters, but the soratami were all androgynous and of a uniform appearance. There seemed to be very little difference between the genders or between individuals within genders.

These two were typically tall and thin. Their pale white skin tended to reflect and magnify any surrounding light, giving them a strange, ethereal glow. Their hair was silver-white and extremely fine. These two wore theirs combed into wild heaps on the tops of their heads, somehow severe and unruly at the same time. Soratami had long, rabbit-like ears that flowed down past their shoulders, but in this case the women had wrapped their ears around their heads like turbans. Dark blue swirls moved along the edges of their ears, folding in on themselves, merging with their neighbors then separating again. Their faces were so impassive they appeared to be ivory masks, but the movement of their facial markings compensated for their otherwise total lack of expression.

The two soratami females lounged on a pair of long couches, a small square table between them. There was a wide, shallow bowl of water on the table in which the image of the academy barge could be seen. Two wizards and several kitsune were visible on the barge's main deck.

At the foot of the couches stood a small and slightly comic figure. He was no taller than a child, rounded and chubby like an overstuffed doll. His skin was a rich blue in color, and when he smiled his fat cheeks bunched up, revealing blinding white teeth. The little blue man floated above the floor of the chamber, and though he stood and the soratami reclined, it was they who were deferential to him.

From bad to worse. The little blue man's voice was cheerful and calm, but his eyes were uneasy. His lips didn't move, and no sound was heard as his thoughts appeared in the soratami minds.

The woman on the left sat up. She was slightly thinner than her counterpart, her face more angular and pinched.

Perhaps, she replied in the same manner as the blue man, mind-to-mind. *But this can still all be turned to our advantage.*

Of course it can. The blue man floated slightly closer to the two women, hovering between them. *It can also mark the end of everything we've done so far. Pull the right thread hard enough and the entire tapestry unravels.*

Hisoka finally got his wish: the princess has come to Minamo. Should we intervene?

We must. Hisoka is a fool, but we cannot not lose sight of the true danger. Even now, the tower at Eiganjo prepares for the worst.

Ha! They have no idea what that means.

No. Forces from both kakuriyo and utsushiyo are massing to attack him in his capital.

If Konda falls . . .

He shall. The only questions are when and what we must do to be ready for it. Ambassador Meloku is still in position?

He is rarely far from Konda's side.

Excellent. Make sure he is ready to move quickly. His situation may become urgent at any time.

And the foxes?

The blue man turned back to the scrying bowl. In it, the academy barge was pulling into the locks at the way station. The harbormaster would perform the proper rituals, and a geyser would carry the ship up to Hisoka's headquarters.

Leave them to the headmaster for now. He knows better than to tell them anything of substance, but monitor him just the same. He has been growing disturbingly skittish lately.

The sharp-faced soratami nodded. *He cannot help but sympathize with his own kind. The humans in Towabara, the learned kitsune on the edge of the forest. Like all academics, he thinks that if he studies the problem long enough, he will arrive at the perfect answer.*

There is no perfect answer. Konda created this problem. We can only manage its impact.

The blue man rotated in the air until he faced the soratami woman behind him, who had yet to contribute to this strange discussion.

Uyo, he said. *You have trained your protégé well. Chiyo is not as powerful as you were at her age, but she is more precise, more elegant. She has benefited greatly from your experience and tutelage.*

Uyo, the silent soratami, demurely lowered her head.

Thank you, O Smiling Kami of the Crescent Moon.

"Please," the blue man said aloud. He smiled wide, his teeth dazzling. "You must call me Mochi." He turned to Chiyo and said, "It would be best if you were there when Hisoka receives the kitsune. Not in plain sight, mind you, but close enough to gauge their mood and intentions. I trust your judgment, but contact us if anything too . . . sensitive comes up. Uyo and I will make sure that the rest of our forces are in place and ready to go."

Without rising from the couch, Chiyo bowed her head, leaning back on her hands. "As you wish, Mochi." She paused then added, "Are things really that far along? Are we on the verge of success at last?"

Mochi smiled again. "A 'verge' is a border," he said. "A single line to be crossed. We are at more of a crossroads, a convergence. The most powerful forces known are all about to occupy the same space. Each will affect the other, and none can predict how. Luckily, we are ready. All possible outcomes can be made to benefit us, if we simply survive the next few days."

Chiyo grinned wolfishly. "Is there any chance we won't?"

The moon kami's eyes twinkled. "There's always a chance. That's what makes life so interesting."

CHAPTER 16

On the border between Towabara and the Sokenzan Mountains, the bandit warlord Godo's world had turned upside-down.

The ogre's curse had worked perfectly at first. Each night, the yuki-onna lured a patrolling sentry or a two-man team down into the valley, where they disappeared. In the morning, their bodies were found, frozen solid with a look of primal terror on their faces. All Godo's men had to do was sit back and watch.

The daimyo's troops were rattled, and the bandits had become bold. With their already limited numbers dwindling, Konda's officers kept sending smaller and smaller patrols. These four- and even six-man teams were easy pickings for Godo's disciplined raiders waiting in ambush. He had counted thirty enemy dead with only light casualties on his own side. Another few weeks and the daimyo would not have nearly enough troops to even patrol this region.

Then things changed. Reinforcements from Eiganjo flowed steadily into the valley for a full day and night. Godo was amazed. He never imagined Konda had so many troops to spare or that he would bother. Instead of a war of attrition that he was bound to win, the warlord now faced open conflict against a larger and better-equipped army.

The yuki-onna claimed still claimed her share each night, but now the hillsides and ridges were thick with Konda's soldiers. The revitalized force had enough manpower to cross the border in force, so Godo's ambush parties were forced to withdraw. The more he pulled his warriors back, the deeper Konda's forces penetrated. They didn't stay to occupy but withdrew at each sunset, leaving nothing of value alive or intact in their wake. Konda's officers began to hang captured bandits from the trees along the ridge line, leaving their bodies to the birds in full view of the valley below. And now this, he thought.

Godo walked alongside his great yak steed, leading it with a leather harness. His spiked club hung beside him from the great beast's saddle. He paced several yards then turned and paced back, keeping his gaze fixed on the baleful discovery his scouts had made only this morning.

A short distance below, among a pile of cracked and broken boulders, lay the body of a sanzoku warrior. His skin was blue. His eyes were wide with terror. His body was covered in a thin layer of frost from the top of his head to the tips of his boots.

Godo grunted, releasing a cloud of white smoke. His yak snorted as if in reply.

Some of his men had already deserted. They were from this region, and their families had been here for generations. They knew what it meant when such a corpse showed up without proper explanation.

Across the valley, on the far side of the hill, Godo heard a great roar. A thousand men cheered with one voice as a huge flaming missile arced up over the hillside. Godo watched it soar over his own head and descend deep into the heart of the foothills, where it exploded in a flash of white fire and gray smoke.

Godo despaired. The daimyo had employed his siege engines to cut off the bandits' retreat. Now that they had tested the range, it was only a matter of time before their infantry massed for a charge. The bandits would either have to stand and fight or retreat into the killing zone where they would be bombarded by Konda's catapults.

The warlord tore his gaze from the fire that the first volley had started and climbed onto his steed. The battle was effectively over. The best he could hope for was to slip away with as many intact warriors as he could. Konda's troops would not have an easy time of it, but there was no way Godo's army could stand against them indefinitely.

In the meantime, the yuki-onna would prey on them all.

As he rode back to his own camp, Godo cursed Hidetsugu again for his treachery. He ought to have known not to accept an o-bakemono at his word. The ogres lived in a world that humans would never understand, and they were a law unto themselves. Hidetsugu was mad, and right now he was probably wracked with uncontrollable laughter at the trick he had played. Godo vowed to visit Hidetsugu some day and enjoy the same kind of laughter at the ogre's expense.

The thought of appealing to his patron kami occurred to Godo, but he didn't think he had enough warm bodies to summon him. The Myojin of Infinite Rage was fickle, and he was as likely to answer prayers with a curse as with a blessing. Still, Godo had to pursue whatever options he could. He had assigned a detail of his more adept bandits to hold a constant vigil of prayer and mediation, beseeching the myojin for his aid. Godo would have welcomed even the slightest sign of recognition, from a ghostly omen to a cleansing wave of fire. He would rather die by the myojin's hand than be captured or killed by the daimyo.

Another triumphant roar came over the hill, and a pair of white-hot fireballs arced into the sky. Godo himself said one last prayer to the myojin before he went to address his men, one last spiteful wish for his most hated enemy.

"Let the akki have their way," Godo whispered.

Above him, another fireball rose into the sky. Godo gripped the yak's reins tightly and guided the shaggy beast down the ridge toward camp.

* * * * *

In the tower of Eiganjo, General Takeno had taken charge.

On the daimyo's orders, he had assembled the finest cavalry unit and a full division of infantry. With their help, he rounded up as many of the Towabara refugees as he could, clearing the entire courtyard of them and their humble belongings. There was some resistance, mostly from fear, but after twenty years of the Kami War, these traumatized people were used to following soldiers' orders. Takeno also ordered runners to move through the streets, announcing that any permanent resident who cared to join the refugees was welcome to do so.

All told, over five thousand people stood at Eiganjo's north gate, shivering, confused, and frightened. The soldiers and horsemen were lined up along the walls on each side of the gate. Takeno climbed into the saddle of his fine white charger and cantered up to the gate.

The sight of the old general quickly silenced the crowd. They were skittish but not stupid. They wanted answers, and Takeno looked official enough to provide them.

"Children of Towabara," he said. His voice carried across the entire crowded courtyard, though every ear still strained to hear, desperate not to miss a single syllable.

"Daimyo Konda has decreed that anyone who can take refuge inside the tower must do so. Those who cannot must be evacuated. The walls of Eiganjo are no longer enough to protect us all."

"What about the kami?" someone screamed.

A nervous muttering swept the crowd, but Takeno's voice rose over it. "These loyal retainers will go with you, to protect you from whatever dangers exist."

"What is that thing in the southern sky?" a woman yelled.

"Why have the kami turned against us?"

"Where are you taking us?"

Takeno waited for the bold shouters to wear themselves out. "There is . . . grave danger to the south. Less so to the east and west. We have decided to go north, to the plains. The daimyo will send for you when it is safe to return."

Takeno looked across the sea of faces. They showed fear, anger, bewilderment, and despair. He wished he had more to offer them.

"That is all," he said. He urged his horse forward and rode back to the front of the tower, ignoring the questions and pleas they hurled after him. As ordered, the officers going with the refugees began opening the north gate.

Takeno followed the tower perimeter until the throng was no longer visible. He turned the corner to the south side of Eiganjo and brought his mount to a stop.

The courtyard was empty—no refugees, no marketplace, no people of any kind. Archers patrolled the parapet atop the outer wall and heavily armored sentries guarded the door into the tower, but the entire area was quiet as a graveyard. Even the great moths circling overhead made no sound.

The guardian dragon Yosei still circled the top of the tower. Konda had somehow communed with the dragon and calmed it down, so it was no longer streaking in circles like a bee trapped in a jar. Now it cruised around the perimeter like a hungry shark, alert and obviously eager for action. Konda's plan was simple: the tower was strong and well defended, with spells in place to fend off the mightiest attacker. Yosei and Konda's army would do battle when the enemy came, and smite him. The citizens of Eiganjo would be safe with their ruler inside his stronghold. The other refugees were at risk outside the walls, but they were safer there than they would be on the battlefield when Yosei met O-Kagachi.

Konda had still not explained what the creature was or how he knew its name. Takeno looked up into the southern sky, which was still slowly filling with the gigantic three-headed form of . . . of whatever O-Kagachi was.

It approached the tower like a great storm cloud, rolling closer inch by agonizing inch. It was far larger even than Takeno had first thought, and the closer it got, the larger it seemed. By the time it reached the tower, it could easily be big enough to swallow all Eiganjo. Perhaps it would prefer to take three big bites, one for each head.

Takeno watched the terrible serpentine form in the sky. It was growing more solid and distinct at it approached, but it was still hazy and ill-defined, as if viewed through wet gauze. Takeno could make out a pattern that appeared to be razor-edged scales along the thing's long necks, and each massive, square head was crowned by two long, pointed tips—horns? Ears?

It made no sound at this distance, but its blurred mouths were constantly open, either roaring or snapping at the air. He felt its presence more clearly than he saw it, prickly waves of force that lapped across the skin on his face like a tide.

Takeno glanced up at Yosei, restrained only by the daimyo's force of will. The general spurred his horse toward the entrance to the tower. The sentries saw him coming and saluted.

Whatever O-Kagachi was, it was coming—and Takeno had sworn to die in the service of Daimyo Konda, for the good of the nation.

Takeno returned the sentries' salute, dismounted, and strode into the tower.

* * * * *

The plains northeast of Eiganjo covered more than ten thousand acres between the forest and the swamp. Arable farmland ran from the northern border of Towabara right up to the walls of the daimyo's tower.

Captain Okazawa of the daimyo's cavalry rode swiftly north through the plains at the head of a five-man unit. They were scouting ahead for the twice-displaced refugees of Towabara, and though he would have preferred to stay and fight, Okazawa was a loyal and true retainer. If his lord ordered him to leap into a pit of poisonous snakes, he would go gladly. If his blood would help preserve the realm, he would open his own veins and die praising the daimyo.

Okazawa saw something in the fields ahead. Without slowing, he narrowed his eyes and peered for a better view.

Hundreds of people were already on the plains, arranged in what appeared to be a large, impromptu camp. They were all sitting or lying down, though the sun was high in the sky behind the yellow haze.

Had other Towabara refugees already fled to the plains? Okazawa quickly explored the possibilities—either they had been there for some time, which meant the plains could support such a large and hungry gathering, or they had arrived recently, which meant there would be competition for whatever resources the plains had. Okazawa hoped he could merge the two groups into one or that they could convince the squatters to move on. The people under Okazawa's protection took precedence over anyone else he might encounter, and he didn't want to force these unexpected guests to fend for themselves if he could avoid it.

Okazawa turned to his lieutenants along side him and jerked his head. They looked forward, nodding as they saw the squatters' camp.

A shocked look crossed the face of his subordinates. The captain signaled for the scouting party to slow down as both lieutenants gestured and pointed in alarm at the camp.

Okazawa followed their gestures and looked again. They were closer now, and he had a clearer view of just who had set up camp in the daimyo's back yard. They weren't sitting or lying down. They were all low to the ground, a horde of thick, stunted figures with stony armored domes on their backs.

Okazawa understood what he was looking at but could not believe it. A horde of akki goblins had circled around Eiganjo and was within a day's march of the tower.

The captain shouted for his scouts to halt and brought his horse to a panicked stop. His heart pounding, Okazawa's head darted from the army of goblins before him back to the mob of Towabara refugees. He wasn't sure he had enough soldiers to defeat this many akki and protect the civilians, but to go back would be certain death for the people as well as a violation of the general's direct orders.

In the distance, the akki began to stir. They unfolded themselves, rising to their full height and stretching their grotesquely long arms. Huge, clawed hands took hold of clubs, cudgels, and other crude weapons. Their demonic, pointed faces slavered and snarled.

A hissing, grating shriek went up from one end of the goblin horde to the other. At the forward edge of the akki mass, two full-sized humans stood. They wore sanzoku bandit gear, and their hair was top-knotted to one side. The man on the left supported the man on the right, who wore a heavy bandage around his shoulder and throat. The daimyo kept all his officers well informed, making sure they could recognize all of the most dangerous bandit chiefs by sight. From an elegant line drawing circulated months ago, Okazawa recognized Seitaro and Shujiro Yamazaki, twin bandit raiders who of late acted as Godo's lieutenants. There was a special price on the brothers' heads, as they had once served Konda but turned against him in the chaos of the Kami War.

Okazawa drew his sword. Bandits and goblins working together, this close to Eiganjo, had made his decision easy before he recognized the twins. He calculated they had roughly twenty minutes before the first goblin invaders reached his position.

"Return to the unit," he told his fastest scout. "Have one

quarter of the infantry stay behind with the civilians. Everyone else should come here, with all available speed, swords drawn and ready to fight."

Okazawa raised his sword. "For the daimyo. For Eiganjo. We have found another war to fight!"

CHAPTER 17

Headmaster Hisoka had prepared a regal reception for the kitsune delegation. As awe-inspiring as the exterior of Minamo was, the entrance hall was even more impressive. The entire school had to be taken in from a distance, but standing on the massive marble staircase beneath the towering silver gate, it was nearly impossible not to feel humbled. Each of the hundred steps was more than thirty feet wide, and the open metal gate was at least one hundred feet tall. They gleamed in the late afternoon sun, thin veins of vibrant blue twinkling against the white marble.

A platoon of twenty student archers stood proudly on the brief courtyard that linked the stairs to the docks, where the geyser delivered incoming visitors. Above the archers on the staircase were a dozen of the academy's top students, mages and adepts from all manner of arcane disciplines. A few stairs above them were the senior staff, the dean of students, the head librarian, and the masters of each individual school of instruction.

At the very top of the staircase stood Hisoka himself, a prim and dapper man with a neat, white mustache and a long, thin beard. He wore radiant blue-and-gold academy robes. Though his face was open and friendly, his eyes were keen and probing. He smiled warmly as Pearl-Ear led her retinue onto the dock.

Hisoka signaled, and three student wizards with long, ornamental horns blew a triumphal note. All the assembled students bowed deeply, archers and wizards alike. The headmaster raised his hands.

"Greetings to you, Lady Pearl-Ear of the kitsune. You are all most welcome guests at Minamo academy."

Pearl-Ear bowed, as did her brother, the three fox samurai, and Pearl-Ear's two "ladies in waiting." Riko looked less conspicuous in her concealing robes than Michiko did, as she was far closer in size to the kitsune. They stayed close enough behind Pearl-Ear to hear her instructions, but not so close that they'd invite attention or comment.

"Many thanks for your warm welcome, Headmaster. You honor us with your hospitality."

Hisoka waved for them to approach. "Please, please," he said. "Enter, and be safe. We have much to discuss. Your soldiers may please wait here—I'm afraid there isn't room enough in my offices for such a large group." Hisoka smiled warmly.

Pearl-Ear straightened. "Of course, Headmaster." She started up the stairs, exchanging a quick glance with Sharp-Ear. They had already decided to leave behind the brothers, Captains Silver-Foot and Nagao, and all the soldiers and rangers. Their job was to escort her to the school, which they had now completed. It would be indecorous to bring armed soldiers into the academy, especially before they had a chance to sound out Hisoka.

Pearl-Ear, Sharp-Ear, Riko, and Michiko mounted the stairs, bowed to students, and exchanged warm pleasantries with the wizards. At the top, Hisoka beckoned them in and bowed deeply from the waist.

"I am glad you are here, Lady Pearl-Ear."

"As am I, Headmaster. This is my brother, Sharp-Ear, and my attendants. They are human, brought here to shore up any deficiencies I may be harboring when it comes to your culture. Sharp-Ear will serve in a similar capacity for the kitsune. I represent all the elders of the great tribes from eastern Jukai, and I have spent decades at Daimyo Konda's court. I am hopeful that among we five—" she bowed to Hisoka—"we will be able to make ourselves understood."

Hisoka nodded. "These are trying times," he said. "It is important that the peaceful tribes of Kamigawa work together."

"Well said, sir. Now, as you say, we have much to discuss. I trust you have no objection to beginning immediately?"

Pearl-Ear kept her large eyes fixed on Hisoka. He returned her stare without any outward sign of concern, his face still open and warm.

"None at all. Follow me to my offices, and we can begin sharing information."

Hisoka turned and clamped his hands together behind his back. "If you will walk with me, Lady," he said, "I will point out some of the more interesting artifacts the school has acquired. If mechanisms don't interest you, we also have a large collection of fine art."

Pearl-Ear hurried for a few paces then fell into Hisoka's rhythm alongside him. "I would be delighted," she said. "That sculpture, there, is that glass, ice, or some sort of enchanted fluid?"

"Ahh," Hisoka said. "That was created by one of my former students. He was quite gifted at the manipulation of . . ."

"He seems friendly," Michiko whispered to Riko. "Can he be trusted?"

They had fallen several paces behind, as appropriate for attendants and convenient for the impostors.

"I think so," Riko replied. "But don't relax. I know he's hiding something, even if he desperately wants to share it. I don't think he's in control here anymore."

"Pearl-Ear said to stay back, stay quiet, and listen," Michiko said. "Do you think we can slip away and do some exploring on our own? You know the layout of the library well enough, don't you?"

"I do," Riko replied, "but we'll have trouble getting in dressed like this. The library here is only for faculty. Students are only allowed in under strict supervision."

"Well, let's stay alert," Michiko said. "If we get the opportunity, I'd like a chance to examine that library."

"I'll be ready," Riko said, "but my hopes aren't high. Shh, we're almost at his offices."

Ahead, Hisoka was extolling the virtues of a new kind of sculpture one of his prize students had invented. Pearl-Ear listened attentively, nodding in all the right places, but she kept looking back to make sure her attendants didn't lag too far behind.

* * * * *

Hisoka's private offices were lined with scroll racks that covered the walls from the floor to the edge of the fifteen-foot ceiling. Every available surface was filled with strange crystalline structures or artistic displays of water and light. The wizard himself sat behind a great wooden desk.

"Headmaster," Pearl-Ear said, "we would like to talk to you about Daimyo Konda."

Hisoka frowned. "Oh? I understood you were here to explore a new level of cooperation between the great tribes and the academy."

"Of course," Sharp-Ear said, "but we must agree that our mutual concerns cannot be addressed without a discussion of the daimyo. His is the largest territory with the most powerful army. He has been at the front of the Kami War since it began."

"As have we." Hisoka stood, pacing as he talked. "The academy was particularly hard hit when the war began. Spirits manifested here before anywhere else nearby. They came in greater numbers and in greater fury. Without the soratami's protection, most of us who live here would be dead by now."

"We honor the sacrifices you've made," Pearl-Ear said. "Nonetheless, all Kamigawa makes similar sacrifices. The answer does not lie in comparing who has shed more blood but rather in discovering the enemy's motivation. Why are the kami attacking us? Why are they so focused here, and on Eiganjo?"

Hisoka shook his head. "This is not a conversation I am willing to have, Lady Pearl-Ear. I am loyal to the daimyo and will not plot against him."

"Plot?" Sharp-Ear shrugged. "Who said plot? We simply wish to explore what connects Konda's tower to this waterfall, where the kami intrusions are most violent."

"Minamo has been a trusted ally of Eiganjo for many years."

"No one is questioning that, Headmaster." Pearl-Ear bowed. "We've no wish to offend or upset you, sir, but we do have information that indicates Daimyo Konda may know exactly why the spirits of the kakuriyo have turned against us. We are merely seeking to know it ourselves. If any place has the resources to decipher our mystery, it is Minamo.

"This is how the kitsune elders have chosen to act: by attacking the root of the problem. We do not have the martial resources to battle kami for the rest of our lives. Many of us are not even certain we should be battling the kami. Perhaps we should instead seek their guidance, ask them what has stirred their ire, and offer atonement."

Sharp-Ear bowed, then locked his eyes on Hisoka's. "What will Minamo do, Headmaster? While Konda's army fights and the kitsune pray, how will the wizards meet this danger that threatens us all? Will you rely on the goodwill of your soratami guardians and continue to train warrior mages for the conflict? Or will you open your archives to us and tell us what you and your learned colleagues know?"

Pearl-Ear dropped to one knee. "You may do both, Headmaster. We are not asking you to betray Konda but to confide in us. This is a place of learning, sir, not a training camp. Help us resolve the spiritual conflict, and you can return to mentoring gifted sculptors and magical prodigies."

Hisoka's eyes were anguished, but his face hung slack like all the muscles had been cut. He looked at Pearl-Ear, then at Sharp-Ear, and he leaned heavily on his desk.

"I cannot help you," he said. "We are willing to begin a more regular exchange between the academy and the kitsune nation. Your knowledge of spiritual magic would make you excellent instructors. We would be proud to enroll your children in whatever course of study appeals to them. And we would love to have your rangers show us the mysteries of Eastern Jukai.

"But that is all I have to offer you now. Perhaps someday, if the situation changes . . ."

"If it does, Headmaster, I fear it will change for the worse," Pearl-Ear said.

"Headmaster," Sharp-Ear said casually. "Why haven't you asked to see our evidence?"

The wizard blinked. "What?"

"We told you we had information that pointed to daimyo Konda. You didn't even ask to see it, or what it was. That's strange behavior for an academic."

Hisoka rose to his full height and said haughtily, "I am loyal to the daimyo. I would not even entertain the idea—"

"I saw you there, Headmaster." Michiko swept forward, pulling her hood back as she came. "On the night I was born. My father did something terrible in the tower of Eiganjo. You were there."

Sharp-Ear's expression did not change, but his ears twitched. Pearl-Ear simply stared, frozen in place, unable to breathe and unwilling to move.

"Michiko-hime." Hisoka paled and staggered. He caught the arm of his desk chair and steadied himself. "Go, all of you go. You have no idea how dangerous it is for you here."

"No, sir, I will not. My father is lord of the nation, but I speak for her people. I am princess of the realm and I demand that you explain yourself. Whatever you did that night has drawn the wrath of the spirit world down upon my people as well as your students. And you will answer for it, now, and help us to undo what you and my father have done."

Hisoka's face reddened and he began to sputter foamy saliva.

"You don't," he choked. "They watch—not safe—go . . ."

Pearl-Ear and Sharp-Ear stepped forward to assist Hisoka. As they took hold of the headmaster's arms and guided him into his chair, the pressure in the room suddenly dropped.

"Sister, dear," Sharp-Ear said. "This is not going well."

Pearl-Ear only nodded. She beckoned Michiko and Riko to come behind Hisoka's heavy desk.

The girls reacted quickly. At this stage everyone in Kamigawa was familiar with the signs of a spirit manifestation. As the kitsune brought the humans down behind the solid shelter of the desk, the air in the room began to swirl, churning countless pieces of paper from Hisoka's files like leaves in a cyclone.

A brilliant arc of light tore through the center of the vortex. It glowed silver-white and thickened, growing wider as each end curled up. The light was almost blinding as the upward curving line parted, revealing a twin row of clean, dazzling teeth.

The light exploded, and everyone behind the desk squeezed their eyes shut as tightly as possible. It burned past the oaken drawers, past their eyelids, and dazzle-blinded them all. For a few moments, all anyone could do was blink and cling to each other.

A cheerful, boyish voice said, "There you are, Princess! I had no idea where you'd gone, but I think I know who took you."

Pearl-Ear and Sharp-Ear recovered more quickly than the humans. They could make out fuzzy shapes and some colors, but for the most part they could only see the world through a bleached white film.

"And to think, after I told you specifically not to come here. I may be a little closer to understanding how the daimyo feels. You never do what he tells you, either."

Sharp-Ear stepped forward. He was unarmed, but his body was tense.

"Who are you?" he said.

The little blue man smiled broadly, his teeth flashing much less violently.

"I am the Smiling Kami of the Crescent Moon," he said. "You can call me Mochi.

"Princess," he said, hopping up on the desk and bowing to Michiko, "I wanted to spare you this experience. But now you're here, and you're asking all the wrong questions. I'm going to have to do something I never wanted to do."

Pearl-Ear slid in beside Sharp-Ear, blocking both the girls and Hisoka from the strange chubby figure perched on the desktop.

Mochi folded his hands behind his back and rocked back on one foot. "You came for answers, didn't you? Well, Hisoka is not in a position to answer. You can see he'd like to be open with you, his new allies, but he physically can't answer you, and I can't let you keep upsetting him in the meantime.

The blue man lifted his arms. Sharp-Ear and Pearl-Ear both growled.

"So. I must step in on his behalf. I'm at your service," the little kami said. "What do you want to know?"

CHAPTER 18

Chiyo walked unchallenged through the halls of Minamo's main building. Most soratami were treated deferentially when they deigned to come down to the academy, but Chiyo carried herself even more aloof. She was slight of build, but her face was severe and her eyes fierce. Even other soratami bowed and stepped aside when she walked by.

Her elevated status was not solely due to her personality. She was one of a small group of soratami prophets, the disciples of Uyo. Under the aegis of the soratami's greatest seer, these women mastered the advanced techniques of astral and thought projection. Uyo herself was thought to be precognitive, but her followers' lesser abilities made them elite even among the mightiest soratami warriors or the most learned diplomats.

She had been monitoring Hisoka's meeting with the kitsune. As soon as Konda's name came up, she had mentally contacted Uyo. No response came, so she continued to listen while she waited. When Michiko revealed herself, Chiyo barely had time to register what had happened before she heard Mochi's jovial voice in her head

Return to Otawara, the blue kami said. *The time has come*

to launch the armada. I will deal with the princess and her kitsune.

Can I be of assistance? Chiyo sent back.

There was a pause. *No,* Mochi said at last. *Telling the simple truth for a change will be refreshingly easy.*

Chiyo turned and quickly headed for the edge of the academy's floating platform. She had a sharp mind and access to the best information, but even she did not know exactly how Mochi planned to achieve his goals. It was enough for her to be able to use her powers to their fullest and establish Uyo's sisterhood as the driving force in soratami culture.

The ground came to an end, and Chiyo paused on the edge overlooking the lake below. She concentrated, and the symbols on her ears started moving so quickly they seemed to vibrate. Chiyo's mouth moved silently, and she steepled her fingers in front of her chest.

The air just off the platform began to thicken as a heavy white cloud gathered. This was how the soratami traveled from their city among the clouds to the world of soil and water below. Only they had learned to summon the clouds and stand upon them as if they were solid. They ruthlessly guarded the knowledge of creating and steering these conveyances, crafting them so precisely that they would not carry anyone other than a true-blooded soratami. To any living thing, from a full-sized human to the smallest gnat, the cloud was merely a cloud and could support nothing more substantial than the heart of a raindrop.

Chiyo stepped onto the billowing white mass. Her feet barely sank into its surface. She willed the cloud to rise, and soon she was floating up past the grand stone spires of the academy, rising high into the evening sky.

She never looked down when she was making this journey, only up. The sky, the stars, the moon above were infinitely more interesting than the tangle of grubby little ants scurrying around on the dirt and the soppy little toads who made their living on the water. Here, high in the sky, she was weightless, she was free, she was ecstatic in the glory of the moon-kissed clouds.

Above her, Otawara loomed, blotting out more and more of the sky as she approached. Soon the soratami would construct more cloud cities across all Kamigawa, floating chaste and serene over the ashes below. Would there be a city for her to rule? She would not rest until it was so.

Chiyo guided the cloud up through the thick layer of white that shielded Otawara from prying eyes below. As her eyes rose over the edge of her home, Chiyo smiled warmly, exulting in the grandeur and glory of the soratami's capital.

It was a true city, not the overgrown village that sprouted up around the falls below. One could walk along its sapphire-blue streets for days, perhaps weeks without reaching the other side. Brilliant white metal arcs supported the towering steel spires that pierced the night sky overhead. Polished granite domes capped museums and grand meditation cathedrals. Silver wire as fine as spiderwebs was woven into intricate patterns that connected building to building and spire to pavement. Under a full moon, the entire city caught and reflected the light, creating a captivating display of shimmering lights and shadows.

It was barely dusk now, but in a few hours the spires, domes, and wire would sing and sparkle under the crescent moon. This architectural marvel would fall dark in few more days, mimicking the moon's own cycle of death, silence, and rebirth. For now, Chiyo simply gazed in satisfaction at the skyline of her home.

Chiyo stepped onto the pavement. From here, this night, the armies of Otawara would ride out and prepare the world for the eventual soratami ascendancy, clearing the soil below of parasites so that cities in the sky above might thrive on the currents of fresh, clean air.

The cloud behind her broke up and began to dissipate. She straightened her robe and started toward the eastern quadrant, where the warriors had massed.

"So this is Otawara," someone said from behind her. "Nice place. A little gaudy, though."

Chiyo's body went rigid. Slowly, she turned, spinning gracefully in place on the balls of her feet. Her eyes filled with tears of rage, and her face became a mask of fury.

You're not supposed to be here, ochimusha.

Toshi inspected his fingernails. "Yes, I had heard that, but you'd be surprised how many places I can go these days."

Chiyo blinked her eyes clear. *I will tear your mind out by the roots.*

"Well, that's up to you. I'd much rather—"

Toshi rolled aside as Chiyo lunged at him. She had produced a sharp silver spike from within her robes, and it made the air sizzle as it whipped past Toshi's ear.

He had his jitte up and ready before she regained her balance. Like a savage, feral cat, Chiyo circled him, her breath hissing through her clenched teeth.

I will kill you. I will kill you and feed your body to the birds.

Toshi straightened up, smiling. He spun his jitte around his fingers like a baton.

"Go ahead," he said. He spread his arms wide. "I'm not going anywhere."

* * * * *

Mochi sat cross-legged on the headmaster's desk. Pearl-Ear, Sharp-Ear, and Riko waited at the far end, with Michiko between them and the kami. Hisoka himself had collapsed in his chair, overwhelmed.

The chubby blue kami waved his hand toward Hisoka. The white-haired wizard's eyes fluttered, and he drifted off into a deep sleep.

"He's had a long day," Mochi explained. "I'd prefer to discuss things with you frankly. Hisoka often requires a more . . . palatable explanation for what he does. With you, I want to speak unfettered."

"Speak, then." Sharp-Ear still regarded the little blue man with extreme suspicion. "Say something of substance."

"I shall. What do you want to know?"

"What did my father do on the night I was born?" Michiko asked.

The moon kami began to rock softly back and forth, an excited grin on his face.

"I've told you that already, Princess. He cast a spell, took something from the spirit world, and trapped it here. It was a very powerful something, very important. The spirit world would like it back."

"Yes, but what *is* it? If it is a kami, what is it the spirit of? What does it represent? Why is it so important?"

Mochi sighed sadly. "This is so much more difficult to explain in words. I'd prefer to show you."

"Show us how?" asked Sharp-Ear.

"Visions, my kitsune friend, visions. My smiling eye looks

down on half the world at a time, night after night. I have seen things and shown things to my believers a million times over. The moon can make you giddy, the moon can make you lonesome. The moon can make you dream." He began rocking again. "Just ask Michiko-hime. I have shown her things before, and they proved to be true."

Pearl-Ear stepped up beside Michiko. "Princess," she said. "Are you willing to put yourself in this strange spirit's hands?"

Michiko nodded. "I am."

"Then we are as well." She bowed to the little blue figure. "Show us your dream, Mochi. If words will not convey the answer we seek, let your power reveal it to us all."

Mochi rocked faster. He opened his eyes wide and flashed his teeth.

Done.

* * * * *

Toshi circled right as Chiyo circled left. She had seemed angry the last time he'd surprised her, but that was nothing compared to now. Rage fairly oozed from her pores. She spat it from her lips and exhaled it from her lungs like poison.

She was fast, too. The jitte was short, hooked, and mostly blunt so it would be effective against bladed weapons.

Chiyo lunged again, slicing through the outer layer of Toshi's sleeve. Even with his lifetime of experience, she was getting through his defenses often enough to make him nervous. She was too proud or too angry to call for help, so at least Toshi only had one exalted demigod to deal with.

He had spotted her outside Hisoka's chambers and recognized

her as one of the soratami who'd attacked him in his own home several months ago. He briefly debated sticking with the kitsune over following the woman, but in the end she seemed most likely to show him something new. He expected the meeting with the headmaster to go on for several hours before they even touched on the important stuff.

Besides, he'd tried to use the Shadow Gate's power to visit Otawara once he'd seen it overhead, but he'd been unable to complete the journey. He'd have to go there in person first, and perhaps not even then would it work.

He'd followed Chiyo in his phantom form and hitched a ride on her cloud ferryboat. It was an odd sensation, a weightless man traveling on an insubstantial platform, but he tended to float anyway in that state, and Chiyo's cloud propelled him along quite nicely.

Now he was here, and she seemed to be having some sort of rage-induced seizure. Every step he took infuriated her more, as if the sound of his sandals on the pavement was appalling. If she got any angrier, her head might simply explode, solving his current problem.

"So," he said. "What do you do for fun here, anyway? Even Numai has a few decent public houses to pass the time. What's a lowlife got to do to get a drink in this town?"

Chiyo screeched, actually screeched like a wounded owl. She sprang at Toshi, hurling her spike at his head with one hand as she drew a second with the other and stabbed for his vitals.

Her attack was rushed and sloppy for her kind. For a nezumi, it would have been a breathtaking display of grace and power, but Toshi had faced much more dangerous opponents, and recently.

He ducked under the thrown spike and parried the other with

his jitte. He clamped his hand around her tiny wrist and stretched both her arms apart, dragging her forward. His face pressed against Chiyo's, nose to nose, as her eyes tried to burn him with the power of sheer hatred. She struggled and kicked, but Toshi blocked her foot with his shin and held her fast.

He winked, drew his head back, and rammed it forward into the bridge of her nose.

Toshi held onto Chiyo's hands as the soratami grunted in pain. She tried to throw herself backward, adding her own momentum to Toshi's blow in the hopes of pulling free, but his grip was too strong. He hauled her to her feet and twisted her wrist until the spike fell from her fingers. Then Toshi stretched her out and butted her again, splattering more thick purplish blood across her delicate features.

He drove his forehead into her face one last time and drew his short sword as she fell. If she were conscious, she could call for help. If she were conscious, he'd have to kill her right here and now.

Toshi took one step before Chiyo's voice ripped through his head like an icy saw.

HELP ME, MY BROTHERS. OTAWARA IS DEFILED.

Toshi's vision fogged, and he staggered to one knee. Chiyo was crawling away from him, her progress slow and painful. She must be tougher than she looked—he wasn't sure about brawling with moonfolk, but if she'd been human her nose would definitely be broken and both eyes swollen shut. If he could just clear his head, he could toss her over the side and take cover until he figured a way out of here.

Toshi fell onto his rear. He sighed and rubbed his eyes, the stinging pain still sharp in his head.

Vague figures rose from the buildings nearby. Toshi counted three, four, more than a half-dozen of them. As they drew closer, he saw tall, thin figures with long, flowing ears and robes flapping in the breeze. They rode atop clouds barely bigger than their feet.

Chiyo continued to inch away from him. Toshi eyed her and the incoming soratami then scrambled to his feet.

Time for him to go. Before he did, though, he wanted to leave the citizens of Otawara something to remember him by. After all, he had no idea when he'd be back.

Toshi fished inside his pack and produced a small red tile. He closed his hand around it, remembering the terrible oni dog Kobo had summoned, the same one pictured on the tile. Toshi opened his hand, placed the tile between his thumb and forefinger, and cracked it in two.

Red mist rose from the pieces of tile. Toshi dropped them to the blue stone pavement and stepped back.

The mist coalesced into a twisted animal shape. A crackling field of red energy danced from one end of the shape to the other, and Otawara's population suddenly increased by one.

The barrel-chested brute was not unlike a dog, but its waist and hindquarters were thin and spindly compared to its massive head and chest. It was covered in thick hide and sharp spikes of bone. The same bony material covered its muzzle and chin, thickening to massive armored plates across its back and shoulders. It had three eyes arranged in a triangle and two sweeping, curved horns. These last two features marked it as an oni, a demonic and malevolent spirit that was hostile to human and kami alike under normal circumstances.

Toshi stepped forward, his hands open and spread wide. He

didn't want to get too close, but neither did he want to break Hidetsugu's injunction to be the first thing the oni saw.

"Here, boy." Toshi waved his hands at the wrist. "You work for me, right?"

The oni dog growled, a booming, dangerous sound that almost bowled Toshi over. He took a step back.

The oni regarded Toshi for a moment. Hot, rank steam puffed from its nostrils. Then, it turned and sniffed after Chiyo. Powerful muscles along its back tensed and it began to pad toward the wounded soratami.

"A gift for you, Otawara," Toshi called to the moonfolk overhead. "From Kobo and the rest of the hyozan reckoners. Tell Mochi he's next."

The dog pounced. Chiyo screamed.

Toshi turned toward a shadow at the base of the nearest building and dived into it.

Michiko had experienced Mochi's visions before, so it was she who recovered most quickly from the initial disorientation.

The princess floated free, her mind and spirit detached from her physical body. Her senses were somehow sharper, as if eyes, ears, and skin were not a conduit for external information but a barrier to it. She was a drop of rain among the thunderclouds, a breath of air in a typhoon wind. She was herself, but she was also a part of something larger, something that she could see and hear and taste without her body.

Though she saw no one, Michiko could feel her friends nearby, Pearl-Ear, Sharp-Ear, and Riko. Of the three, Pearl-Ear seemed the most tranquil.

Behold the spirit realm, Mochi's voice said.

Michiko looked out onto the swirling mass of dust and energy, recognizing it as the kakuriyo Mochi had shown her before. She wished she could communicate with Pearl-Ear and the others, but she couldn't even hear her own voice.

This is the spirit realm, Mochi said. *Separate from your world but inextricably linked. Every physical thing in the utsushiyo has a spiritual reflection in the kakuriyo. Or perhaps every spirit here has a physical reflection there. No matter how you look at it, our homes are both remarkably similar and remarkably distinct.*

In your world, Mochi continued, *spirits dress themselves in physical bodies and can be drawn to specific locations through prayer and ritual. Here, they are defined not by their form but by their essence. Everything that exists here overlaps something in the solid world. The beings here live in an exalted state, free from the physical maladies of disease, decay, and death. A thing from the utsushiyo will inevitably wither and fall away, but its essential nature, its spirit, lives on in the kakuriyo.*

The vast, roiling void began to divide, forming two identical halves of an enormous whole. On the one side, rocks and trees and rivers took shape; on the other, spectral reflections of the landscape shimmered into view, a perfectly symmetrical world split down the center by a hazy line.

This is why the kami that make war upon your world are so alien and strange. They were never meant to manifest so completely, so quickly, under the stress and strain of rage. Our worlds are connected, but there is great distance between them. Traversing that distance is horrendously difficult, and nothing that pierces the veil between substance and spirit does so unchanged. Think of it as diving through a wall of thorns—you are still you when you emerge from the opposite side, but your outer shape is changed, even to the point of rendering you unrecognizable. You are still you, but you are bleeding, half-blind, and twisted by pain. The realms were not meant to interact this way. Indeed, they could not until Daimyo Konda found a way to breach the barrier.

The more solid half of the realm began to fade from view,

even as its ghostly counterpart glowed more brightly. The edge of the kakuriyo became more distinct, circling the border of the spirit realm like half-frozen river filled with sharp shards of ice. Wisps of smoky energy trailed through the barrier, disappearing and returning like a needle and thread through heavy fabric.

The mages and adepts of Kamigawa have always been able to do wondrous things by tapping into the power here. The kitsune chant that grows crops, the healer's balm that closes wounds, the warrior's prayer that summons courage—all these things are possible only because of the spirit realm and the essential energy it contains. This is the source of all magic in the utsushiyo, of all magic anywhere. It is the vital force that makes life and conscious thought possible.

All along the scaly border, heat and light and smoke rose to the barrier, disappeared, and returned at some distant point along the barrier. There was a natural bleed between the two realms, an exchange of essential substance that kept the two worlds in balance.

Your father was not content to seek the spirits' blessing before he accessed their power. He bypassed the natural order of things and seized a powerful spirit himself, with his own hands, binding it to his world and his will. In doing so he created a rent in the veil between our worlds, a rift that angry kami have been widening with each new attack. But in taking direct action in your world, we become vulnerable to it as well. Just as our power affects your world, your worship affects our power. The more we interact with the physical world, the more like its native residents we become.

I cannot speak for the great myojin, but I do know that we kami, we lesser spiritual entities, form attachments to the white-water rapids that thundered down the hall toward the attackers.

For a moment, nothing else happened, and Hisoka prayed that the deluge had swept the invaders all the way out the main gate and over the side. His prayer withered before he could complete it as a half-naked savage with face paint and a skullcap appeared, bounding sideways from wall to wall up the hallway, completely avoiding the rushing river the mages had summoned.

The savage crossed the distance to the wizards in four prodigious leaps. Hisoka cried out as the invader's sword erupted from between the shoulder blades of the tallest mage. The wild man kicked another wizard in the throat, spun in mid-air, and decapitated the last water mage with his sword. As the head fell, the torrent of water subsided and began flowing back toward Hisoka. The last surviving wizard slumped to the ground, his back to the sodden wall, his hands clutching at his crushed windpipe.

The headmaster took one last look at the evacuation, so nearly complete. Hisoka stiffened his spine, straightened his robes, and strode forward to meet the invaders.

With each step his legs grew heavier, and the painful ball in his stomach twisted. The savage stared at him as he approached. The invader's bloody sword was still in his hand, but as Hisoka came into range, the painted warrior stood aside and allowed him to pass.

The waters were now down to Hisoka's knees. Robbed of the minds that summoned it, the water seemed to hesitate, unsure of which direction to flow.

Something very large was splashing through the stream ahead. Compared to the sound of his own feet in the deluge, whatever approached was either twice as large or had twice as many feet.

Hisoka's jaw dropped when the ogre came into view. He couldn't help himself, couldn't speak—he could only stare up at the battle-mad face of evil leering down at him. The ogre's chin was slick with blood, and he carried several arrows in his chest and shoulders. If they troubled him, he gave no sign.

"Oh, splendid," the o-bakemono said. "He looks important."

Hisoka found his voice. It was thin and carried no force behind it, but it was better than simply staring in terror.

"I-I am Hisoka," he stammered. "H-Headmaster of this school." He started to bow reflexively but stopped himself. "I will surrender to you on one condition: that you spare the remainder of my students and staff."

The ogre tilted his head. "No deal," he said. "I don't need your surrender, and the lives of everyone here are already forfeit."

In a flash, the huge brute had seized Hisoka around the waist with one hand. The ogre lifted the headmaster to eye level, coughed, and spat in Hisoka's face.

"For Kobo," the ogre said. He opened his mouth wide and shoved Hisoka's head between his jaws.

The last thing the headmaster saw was slavering, blood-stained teeth. He said one final prayer on behalf of his students and one last curse for the Smiling Kami of the Crescent Moon.

The ogre clamped down. Hisoka's vision went black as he heard a terrible, sickening crunch.

* * * * *

Hidetsugu cast the headless body into the ebbing flow of water, where it bobbed like a cork.

Farther down the hall, his lead yamabushi was returning from the large chamber at the end. He held up five fingers, shook his head, and dragged the edge of his palm across his throat.

"Good," Hidetsugu said. "That's this level cleared. Come. There are many more floors above."

The yamabushi nodded and sprinted past the ogre. Hidetsugu glanced down at the headmaster's body.

All things considered, he still would have preferred to have Kobo with him, but avenging his apprentice was proving almost as invigorating as training him. In the end, Chaos would consume them all. Before that happened, however, he planned to leave this school, the city overhead, and the waterfall itself in a charred, smoking hole littered with rubble and bodies.

Hidetsugu splashed on through the water. Spitefully, he trampled Hisoka's body as he followed the flow of water down the hall, moving toward the main staircase at the center of the building.

Plenty of work left to do here, he told himself. The ogre licked his lips and smiled.

CHAPTER 26

General Takeno stood before Konda in the daimyo's private chamber. Konda himself had his back to Takeno, fixed as usual on the steaming stone disk at the far side of the room.

Takeno had his hand on his sword and his ear cocked as he listened down the short staircase. Konda had hailed him when he came in, but the daimyo had not yet turned to face his oldest and most trusted retainer. The general had tried to inform Konda about what was developing just outside the tower walls, but the daimyo would hear none of it. His strange eyes never left the disk, and when Takeno spoke Konda only repeated that he had absolute faith in his prize.

So the general stood, waiting for the inevitable. O-Kagachi had torn through Eiganjo's defenders like a scythe through wheat. If the tower's magical defenses did not hold, the great Towabara nation would end here, today, on this dusty patch of mist-shrouded ground.

Takeno was sad, tired, and numb. Fighting beside his lord, dying along with Konda would have been enough. Standing forgotten while the daimyo communed with his totem was hardly a noble death for a veteran warrior.

A stupendous boom sounded outside, and the entire tower shuddered. Takeno imagined O-Kagachi prodding and testing the tower the way he had tested the walls of the fortress, with multiple blows from his multiple jaws clamped tight. Another boom, another shudder, and mortar dust rained down from the ceiling.

"My lord," Takeno said, "the great serpent has come."

"Let him come," Konda said without turning. "He will never breach Eiganjo, and he will never claim my prize."

"He has already broken the outer walls," Takeno said softly.

Now Konda did turn. His eyes lingered on the statue. "So? It is the tower now that will protect us, the tower that has been engineered for just such an event."

Takeno swallowed then shook his head. "No, my lord. I don't think even the architects of Eiganjo imagined a nightmare like this. Most of your kingdom is already in ruins, thanks to the Kami War. The bulk of your citizens are crammed into this tower like arrows in a quiver. If O-Kagachi breaks through, you, your kingdom, and your people will all be at risk."

Konda narrowed his wandering eyes. "Are you questioning my orders, General?"

"I am, my lord, but with good reason. I have never fully understood what it was we did on that night so many years ago." He gestured to the stone disk. "I have seen how that has made you powerful, but it has also brought the wrath of the entire kakuriyo down upon us. O-Kagachi is the ultimate expression of that wrath. Is that piece of stone worth all that we have fought for and lost?"

Konda looked troubled. "You disappoint me, General. I thought you, of all people, would remain true no matter what hardships we faced."

"I am true, my lord, but I am convinced that we will die here—you, I, everyone in the tower. That conviction has loosened my tongue. Unlike you, I am an old man, at the end of my life. Now that I am to die, I crave a boon: Tell me what I am dying for."

"You are dying for the nation," Konda said. "Exactly the same as you would expect from any of your riders, from any of the retainers who have sworn to serve us. This—" he waved his hand back at the statue—"is the future of our land. It is power made solid, and it enriches any who understands its nature. It is a piece of the spirit world, that divine spark that crosses the line from immaterial to material. As such, it calls to the kami and myojin, who grow diminished by its absence and seek to reclaim it.

"I say my people, my nation is more deserving of its blessings. We—" he gestured between Takeno and himself—"are more deserving. That is what war has always been about, General: the treasures at stake and who benefits from them. If Godo knew it existed, he would come for it with all of his bandit horde, and we would fight him off. How is the Kami War any different?"

"Godo is but a man, my lord, and the people used to worship the spirits."

"Now," Konda said, "they no longer have to. We are above the kami now. We bear the very thing that made them exalted. Now we are exalted, and they must worship us."

Takeno did not reply. He stared, his face a mask.

Konda sneered. "Go if you wish, General. I will not ask of you what I am not prepared to do myself." He turned back to the statue. "I will stay. If O-Kagachi tries to touch my prize, I will fight him to the death." He turned his back and raised his hands to the stone disk. "If you truly believe that I have led us all to our deaths here, you must strike me down. If you have another course to pursue, usurp my position and lead in my place. I have no friends left—not you, not Isamaru, not even my own daughter. Strike now, Takeno, if you think it will save Towabara. I will not resist."

A terrific blow struck the exterior wall, knocking both men to their knees. More dust fell, along with splinters of wood from the ceiling beams and small chunks of stone.

Takeno rose, crossed the room, and bowed to Konda. "I will never leave you, my lord, never abandon you. It is my oath and my destiny to fight at your side, but it is also my desire."

Konda put his hand on the general's shoulder. "It is a difficult thing, to lead." Konda pulled Takeno close and embraced him. "Especially when only you can see how treacherous is the path ahead."

O-Kagachi struck the tower again, and this time Takeno felt the entire building sway like a sapling in a stiff breeze. He and Konda managed to stay on their feet by propping each other up. Miraculously, the stone disk remained fixed on its pedestal, the fetal serpent on its face lifeless and inscrutable.

"I believe the outer wall has given way, my lord." Takeno retrieved his sword from the floor. "We may have to fight. Have you a weapon?"

Konda waved his concerns aside. "Noble General," he said, "I have the loyalty of my retainers. I have the love of my people. I have the prize that stirred the entire spirit world to action. I need nothing else."

"Very good, my lord."

The tower shuddered once more from another tremendous impact, and the walls around the short staircase collapsed. Beyond the rubble, Takeno could see that other interior walls had crumbled, turning this level of the tower into one great chamber enclosed only by the solid stone and enchantments of the tower's exterior. Through the dust, Takeno could see a hole in that massive barrier and the night sky beyond the hole.

The exterior wall buckled, exploding inward as if struck by a black powder bomb. Takeno saw a wedge of sharp rock as large as a table slicing through the air toward Konda. Though the daimyo was facing the deadly missile, his eyes had migrated to the far left and right of their sockets, trying to stay fixed on the stone disk.

Takeno sprang forward without hesitation. With his sword held high and his powerful voice echoing across the chamber, he leaped into the path of the soaring stone and slashed at it, splitting a jagged piece from its surface.

The rock plowed into the old soldier's chest, bearing him violently backward. Takeno's weight and momentum were sufficient to deflect the great chunk of wall away from Konda. As he sailed past his lord and master, Takeno tried to cough out one last warning, one final word of caution in the hopes it would keep Konda alive for just a little while longer. His lungs were flat and his back was broken. The stone missile drove him out the opposite wall, crashing through the rocks and arcing over the north courtyard below.

His last thoughts were those of a soldier who had done his duty.

* * * * *

Konda whirled as Takeno's body flew past him, borne on a bier of jagged stone. He was as shocked by the sight of his loyal subordinate's broken body as he was by the force of the impact against the far wall. There was a deafening crack and an avalanche of stone cascading down to the ground.

Konda turned to his prize. Laboriously he dragged his eyes away from it and scanned the wreckage around him.

There were holes in both sides of the exterior wall. No whole walls stood anywhere on this level of the tower. Takeno was gone. His armies outside had either been defeated or driven off. Below Konda, thousands of people huddled together, praying for death to pass them by.

Something glittered on the far side of the tower, out in the cool night air. Konda took a step toward it, unsure of its size or shape but fascinated by the palpable aura of power that rolled off it like heat from a furnace.

Outside the hole, O-Kagachi's eye blinked, and the great serpent roared, sending a jet of hot, acrid breath blistering through the chamber. Konda shielded his face with his forearm.

So this is how it ends, he thought. The oldest and most powerful spirit from the kakuriyo come to make war on the oldest and most powerful ruler from the utsushiyo. It would have been unthinkable twenty years ago, a ridiculous concept. But as Konda told Takeno, he had the love of his people, the loyalty of his soldier, and the power of his prize.

With the stone disk in his possession, Konda could be fearless. He alone knew what it represented, how its power could humble even O-Kagachi. It had made him immortal. It had made him invulnerable. Now he would use it to destroy the beast that threatened to undo all he had built.

Konda turned to face the prize. His eyes were drawn straight to it, as always, but he also noticed something on the periphery. The daimyo froze, nearly paralyzed by cold and unimaginable rage.

Someone was standing next to the stone disk's pedestal. He was an average-looking man, armed with samurai swords and dressed in simple black linen. His dark hair was pulled tight behind his head.

"So," the warrior said. "This is it. The Taken One." He placed his hand on the closest edge of the disk and quickly drew back as if stung. "It's cold," he said then shrugged. "It's not that impressive."

"Take your hand away, sir." Konda's voice could not have been more menacing if he'd had a sword to the young man's throat. For the first time in years, his eyes stopped listing and fixed firmly on the intruder.

Konda noticed Takeno's sword on the floor and quickly scooped it up. "You will die for this. Draw, if you care to, and defend yourself."

The young man shook his head. "No, daimyo," he said. "We will not fight."

Behind Konda, more of the exterior wall blew inward as O-Kagachi widened the hole. The daimyo felt grit and sharp stones along his back, but he did not wince, and he did not waver.

He stepped forward, pointing the tip of Takeno's sword at the intruder. "Who are you?"

The intruder smiled. "I am oath-brother to both ogre and rat. I am the bane of snakes and the shivering cold that baffles moonlight. I have walked the streets of the cloud city and crawled through the mire of Numai.

"I am Toshi Umezawa, sir. I am the man who twice stole your daughter. I have come here now to steal this thing that you value so much."

* * * * *

Toshi had never seen the daimyo up close—hardly surprising, since a man in his position was obliged to avoid government officials whenever possible. He had thought Konda would be older, more bent and wizened. He also wondered what had happened to the daimyo's eyes, which seemed to big for his head and somehow vibrated as he glared at Toshi.

When Toshi said the word "steal," Konda charged. The ochimusha didn't expect the daimyo to be so fast, but he still had time to slide behind the cover of the stone disk.

The daimyo yelled something incoherent about glory and destiny and the future as he wildly swung his sword. Toshi was far more concerned about the huge face outside that was dismantling the wall brick by brick than he was about the frenzied daimyo.

He had watched Konda and the other old man for a short while, long enough to confirm his long-held suspicion: He didn't like Konda. Besides the fact that he had started the Kami War and imprisoned his own daughter, the old man was selfish. Clinging to the stone disk at the expense of everything else, keeping it locked away in this dank little chamber—what was the point in ruling the entire spirit world by stealing something if all you were going to do was sit and stare at it? He claimed it was a source of power, but even the akki and the nezumi knew that power unused was power wasted. Maybe no one else could have taken the disk from the spirit world, but Konda was definitely someone who didn't deserve it.

Toshi realized that Konda was still yelling at him. That proves it, he thought. Truly formidable leaders don't have to yell to get their point across. Uramon never yelled. Hidetsugu . . . well, Hidetsugu roared a lot, but he was confident enough to let his actual words convey his threats rather than the volume at which he said them.

"How will you move it, thief?" Konda was raving, still slashing wildly with his sword, pursuing Toshi in an undignified scramble like one child chasing another around a tree. "The prize is mine, mine alone, and I will kill you before I ever let you touch it again."

Toshi stayed ahead of Konda, circling around the pedestal. What a blowhard, he thought. *This* is the noble and respected ruler of Eiganjo? Michiko's father was little more than a cranky old man, a miser who had forgotten the value of treasure and concerned himself only with keeping it from others.

The tower trembled once more, and the great serpent finally worked one of his heads through the hole in the outer wall. Time to finish this. Toshi veered away from the stone disk, moving toward the center of the room. He drew both his swords, watching Konda with one eye and O-Kagachi with the other.

Though old and manic, Konda did not seem to have exerted himself at all during the chase. His eyes rattled around in his skull like marbles in a cup, and his breath blew his thin mustache around, but he was still focused and vibrant.

"Stand and fight, ochimusha. It's better to die on General Takeno's sword than to be crushed and consumed by the great serpent."

Toshi lowered his swords, his face thoughtful. "That's good advice," he said. "If I were you, I'd take it."

The ochimusha called out to his myojin and endured the stinging burn on his arm as he faded from sight.

Konda fairly howled as Toshi disappeared. The daimyo ran to where Toshi had stood, slashing the empty air. Standing nearby, invisible, intangible, Toshi shook his head. How did this loon ever rule Kamigawa?

Too late, Konda realized he was now in direct line of sight with O-Kagachi. The great beast roared, shaking more stones loose from the crumbling tower. Konda, to his credit, stood firm as he called out defiantly.

"Here I am, guardian of two worlds. What you seek is behind me. Come and take it, if you can." He paused, glancing over his shoulder, displaying his wandering eye. "You, thief, hidden in the shadows. Do your worst. The glory of Eiganjo will last forever."

Toshi faded in alongside the pedestal. "Maybe," he called. "Maybe not." He reached out and placed his palm on the stone disk. As before, some strange force jolted him, shocking him like a frozen piece of metal, but he did not retract his hand.

Staring intently at the shadow of the pedestal, Toshi willed himself to fade once more. He concentrated on his palm and the stone disk beneath it. The great round mass grew transparent, a ghostly image of itself, then it, too, disappeared.

Konda screamed. O-Kagachi plowed through the shattered rooms and walls that had once been the daimyo's private chambers.

Guiding the stone disk like a child's balloon, Toshi stepped into the pedestal's shadow and left the noise and the strife of Eiganjo behind.

CHAPTER 27

Toshi hung motionless in a sea of empty black space. Usually the journey through shadows lasted only a few seconds, but he had ground to a halt halfway between his origin and his destination.

Disoriented, Toshi jerked his head around until he spotted the daimyo's prize floating nearby. He quickly calmed down as his surroundings becoming more familiar.

He had been here before when he first accessed the power of the Shadow Gate. Then he had been forced to float until he called upon his myojin. It was her power that he employed when he moved through shadow. Perhaps this was her way of inviting him to another discussion.

"Myojin of Night's Reach," he said, though his voice was lost in the soundless void. "I am in haste. Come forth and talk to me."

Toshi, the myojin's cold voice came. *I see you have returned. You have brought something new . . . and left your manners behind.*

"Forgive my impertinence. As you noted, I am bearing a unique burden."

Indeed. That is something we need to discuss. Look up.

Toshi craned his head back and was borne up by the myojin's power. Once more he hurtled toward a small white speck in the distance that grew larger as he approached.

Toshi hit the hard white floor of the myojin's honden. He quickly got to his feet, noting the daimyo's statue standing on its edge nearby. The etched figure of the serpent faced him, impassive and immobile as ever.

He stood and faced the curtain and the cloud of hands. The myojin's bone-white face was slowly fading into view at the center of the broad black field.

She stared at him for a moment. *What have you there?*

"This is some sort of spirit," Toshi said, "which Daimyo Konda wrenched from the kakuriyo."

It is that. It is also so much more.

Toshi paused. "So Mochi told us. Where do you stand, O Night, on Mochi as an ally?"

The cold face continued to stare. It was so lifelike, so close to motion that Toshi began to grow uneasy under its gaze.

He has his uses, the myojin said at last.

"He presented his interests as if they were yours," Toshi said. "As if you and he had an understanding."

More silence. Toshi cleared his throat. "Is there one?"

I have understandings with many entities, Toshi. In your world, in the spirit realm, and in other worlds far beyond both.

"Of course. But . . ." He broke off. "I do not wish to offend you again."

Sometimes, acolyte, you are too clever for your own good. Speak.

Scott McGough

"Mochi has designs on this." He pointed to the stone disk. "As do I, but I must admit, all that I have accomplished . . . including the acquisition of this . . . is because of you. I know I cannot keep it without your support.

"If you intend to relieve me of this—if you've promised it to Mochi or if you just want it for yourself—I would prefer to just hand it over now. Don't have me removed or stranded in the void or fed to a primal spirit beast. I want it, but I haven't really decided what I'm going to do with it yet. If you have, I will humbly surrender it to you.

"However, if it please you, O Night, leave it to me. Let me have it because I want to keep it from Mochi. Let me have it because if I do figure out something grand to do with it, I will do it in your name and according to your desires. I am not known for my steadfastness, O Night, and perhaps I am not trustworthy, but I would be dead ten times over if not for your blessings, and so I rededicate myself to your cause and your glory."

The cold bone mask lost all sense of vitality, becoming no more alive than an actor's mask. Toshi waited, becoming convinced that the myojin had abandoned him and left him to wait forever.

What a fine speech, Toshi. I would be truly moved by your eloquence and your passion except for one thing: I have no interest at all in the daimyo's prize. I don't care if Mochi has it, I don't care if you have it. So long as you never use the Shadow Gate to transport it through my realm again, you may do as you will. Which, my acolyte, is what I suspect you were always intending to do.

Toshi blinked. "Really? I can have it?"

Of course. But I do not want it here. Anywhere it goes,

*O-Kagachi will follow. And avoiding his presence here is some-
thing I do care about.*

Toshi pondered for a moment. "Where is he now?"

*Would you like to see? Mochi isn't the only one who can pro-
duce visions. Dreams are my messengers, too, after all.*

Toshi glanced back at the prize. "You can show me Eiganjo?"

I can.

"You can show me Minamo?"

I can.

Toshi smiled. "Show me, then."

The white mask's empty eyes flashed, and Toshi felt himself
being drawn into them.

* * * * *

Daimyo Konda kneeled in the wreckage of his private
chamber. There was no roof over Konda's head, barely any
walls around him, and the wind blew his long hair and whiskers so that they stretched parallel to the ground. He still held
Takeno's sword listlessly in his hand, the tip lodged between
two floorboards.

Eiganjo still stood, though it had been badly battered by the
Great Old Serpent. O-Kagachi had withdrawn when the statue
disappeared, but not before tearing the top off the tower. Without
his prize to defend, the daimyo seemed lost, broken, humbled.
Without the prize to pursue, O-Kagachi had slowly turned his
vast bulk and slithered away, fading from sight before he had
cleared the exterior walls.

Konda stood, slowly, and shuffled to the edge of the chamber,
which now overlooked a straight drop to the courtyard below.

Takeno's sword cut curls of wood from the floor as it dragged behind him.

The terrible, clinging mist that had shrouded Eiganjo had finally dispersed, allowing the daimyo to see clearly the devastation O-Kagachi had created. Broken stones, broken bodies, and a hundred small fires littered the ground. Konda straightened his shoulders, sheathed Takeno's sword, and buried his head in his hands, weeping.

From below the wreckage of the short staircase came a voice. "My lord?"

Konda lifted his face. He composed himself, wiped his eyes, and called, "I am here. Who calls?"

"This is Captain Okabe. We are working to clear the rubble away. We should be able to reach you before long. Are you hurt, my lord?"

Konda didn't answer. He walked across the floor, his drifting eyes still drawn to the empty pedestal. At the top of the ruined staircase, he called, "Carry on with your work. I await your swift arrival."

Konda tightened the belt on his robe and stood at attention. When they found him, he would not be bent and weeping like an old man. He would be standing tall and proud, like the lord of the realm.

"My lord."

The voice came from behind Konda. Startled, he whirled in place. A pale figure stood at attention, a soldier with gleaming white armor and an empty scabbard belted on his hip.

Konda could not hide his shock. "Takeno?"

The ghostly figure was almost a perfect copy of the man Konda had seen killed minutes before. He looked different now, his hair, skin, clothes and boots all bone-white. It was not the Takeno who had served Konda so faithfully for so long. His eyes were featureless white orbs that never blinked. His face was a twisted, half-melted parody of what it had been in life. He had grown taller, broader, with one arm far more massive and muscled than the other. His sword was in his hand, but Konda could not see a clear distinction to mark where the ghostly hand ended and the pale weapon began.

"My lord," the ghost said again, "I am ever your loyal retainer." The phantom bowed and held out his smaller hand, which seemed shriveled and dead compared to the bulging power of his sword arm.

Konda glanced at the spectral hand then back to the empty scabbard on the ghost's hip. Cautiously, he drew Takeno's sword and offered it hilt-first to the shade of its owner.

The shade of Takeno ignored the weapon it had carried in life and saluted with the blade attached to his arm. He stood. "What are your orders, my lord? We are all sworn to your service."

"We?" Konda stared at the blank-eyed ghost as he swept past him, moving once more to the precarious edge of the floor.

The courtyard below was now full of ghostly warriors, mounted on white spectral horses and arranged in huge, precise formations. Each was swollen, or stunted, or somehow distorted from the lean, trim figures created by Konda's daily drills. Some had no eyes at all, some had horn-like protrusions jutting from their shoulders, and others had distended, scissor-like jaws.

A standard bearer carried Konda's banner high at the head of the assembly. Spectral horses whinnied. Disturbing half-man, half-moth creatures joined at the saddle soared silently through the sky around the daimyo's position. Konda stifled a shudder whenever he saw one clearly—they were enough like his former retainers to stir feelings of remorse in the man who had ordered them to their deaths but monstrous enough to also raise his disgust. O-Kagachi had done far worse than kill his army: The Great Old Serpent had ruined them, for the next world as well as this one.

As one, the ghostly warriors raised their weapons and cheered Konda's name.

Takeno slashed the air with his sword behind the daimyo, and the ghost army fell silent.

"Your orders, my lord?" the general's shade repeated.

A cruel smile crossed Konda's face. Eiganjo was not beaten after all, and neither was he.

"First," Konda said, "we are going to take back what is rightfully mine." He raised his arms triumphantly and was rewarded with a ghostly roar of approval from his army.

"Then," he said, "we will cleanse Kamigawa of this kami plague once and for all."

* * * * *

Toshi was looking at Minamo academy, floating level with the school's foundation two hundred yards away.

"What was all that?" he said. "All those ghosts and the daimyo? I've heard of heroes becoming kami spirits before, but never five thousand at once."

O-Kagachi was never meant to manifest in the utsushiyo, Night's voice said. *In a sense, he is the utsushiyo. He presence disrupts the basic fabric of wherever he appears. Those men all swore solemnly to serve Konda. They were killed by*

O-Kagachi. Perhaps he anchored their spirits to Eiganjo and its ruler.

Toshi nodded. "I bet that stone thing had something to do with it, too. Konda's eyes are still funny."

Indeed. Look quickly, Toshi. I will not stay here long.

"But I need to see the inside."

Where Mochi is. You may be at odds with him, but I have no interest in confronting him.

"Yet. Okay, then." Toshi looked.

The building and grounds were silent and still. There was no sign of Hidetsugu or the yamabushi he'd brought with him. From the damage and the blood at the entranceway, it seemed certain that they had been here. Toshi didn't imagine the ogre would leave without some grand, destructive gesture.

Overhead, something screeched and rattled. Toshi glanced up toward Otawara and stifled a yelp.

The space between the academy and the soratami's cloud city was completely filled by a cloud of snapping, slavering mouths. Above the cloud, two huge horns as tall as buildings curved up into the moonlit sky. Three massive eyes glared malevolently down upon the school.

"That's Hidetsugu's oni," Toshi hissed.

Yes.

"I'd like to go now. Back to your honden."

Of course.

* * * * *

Toshi came back to himself on the white floor, facing the myojin's mask.

"Okay," he said. "I need to hurry."

Go with my blessings, acolyte, and take that thing with you.

Toshi nodded. He laid his hands on the daimyo's prize, turned to the myojin, and said, "You know where I'm going?"

I do. And I expect I know where you'll be after that. If I have need, I will contact you.

"Thank you." Toshi stood up straight, and then bowed deeply from the waist. "You honor me, O Night."

Flatterer.

Toshi put his hands on the disk once more and concentrated, fading from sight.

CHAPTER 28

"We can't stay here." Sharp-Ear was pacing nervously in front of Hisoka's office door.

"We can't leave," Pearl-Ear said. "Out there is where the enemy is."

"In here is where they're headed. Surely we can find a way past them?"

"I believe we could, but Michiko and Riko would have a much harder time."

Sharp-Ear turned to the girls. "What do you say? Care to make a run for your life?"

Michiko shook her head. "I know you don't trust Toshi . . . and perhaps I don't, either . . . but I do believe him. The ogre is out for blood. Toshi is his oath-brother. He can protect us."

"But he's not here, Princess." Sharp-Ear anxiously twisted the end of his tail. "The longer we wait, the more certain it is that the ogre will find us and the more certain Mochi here will thaw out. Also, the o-bakemono might just a cast a spell and wreck the building. Has anyone thought of that? Toshi can't talk the building out of falling on us."

"Sure I can." The ochimusha stepped from the same shadow

he'd used only a few hours ago. He only came partially into the room, however, his left arm and leg still hidden in the darkness beyond. "I can talk anyone into anything. I talked you into waiting, didn't I?"

"And we've waited long enough," Sharp-Ear said. "If you can do something to help, do it."

Toshi didn't answer. He looked at Mochi and said, "How's he?"

Pearl-Ear said, "As you left him."

"Good." Toshi came all the way into the room, carrying the huge stone disk in one hand. "I brought something for him."

Pearl-Ear gasped. Riko and Sharp-Ear stared wide-eyed, and Michiko fixed Toshi with a penetrating stare.

Toshi glanced back at the stone disk as if he had forgotten he was carrying it. "It's not me," he said. "I used a touch of shadow to make it weightless." He raised and lowered the stone disk as if it were no more than a dinner plate. "See? Give it a try, I bet you could—"

"That is what my father took from the kakuriyo," Michiko said grimly.

"And I took it from your father." Toshi crossed the room and set the daimyo's prize down next to Mochi. "There," he said. "If Mochi stays cold long enough, Hideo and the All-Consuming Oni of Chaos can wrestle Konda and O-Kagachi for the right to swallow him whole."

Michiko was moving toward the stone disk, extending her hand. "I've never seen it in person before."

"Don't touch it," Toshi and Pearl-Ear said together. Michiko looked at them, wounded, and Toshi added, "Your father touched it and it changed him."

Pearl-Ear nodded. "It was also created by a spell that used you as a mystical fulcrum. This thing is tied to you somehow, Michiko, and it may be dangerous, especially to you."

Michiko lowered her hand. "Yes, sensei."

Sharp-Ear was strolling around the disk and Mochi. "So you're just going to leave it here?"

"I am. I have it on good authority that O-Kagachi will come for it again as soon as he figures out where it is."

"He will destroy Minamo," Riko said.

Toshi grunted impatiently. "He'd better hurry, if that's his plan, because Hidetsugu won't leave much behind." He turned to the others. "Who wants out of here before that happens?"

* * * * *

One by one, Toshi carried the princess and her friends away from the deathtrap that was Minamo. At Pearl-Ear's request, he ferried them to the edge of the wild kitsune village in East Jukai.

They were relieved to be safe but not as relieved as he was. He spent the last few trips in a cold sweat, expecting to see disembodied jaws or golden serpentine heads as big as a mountain appearing at any moment. Or worse, he could be spotted by Hidetsugu, who would insist that Toshi join in the bloody reckoning he was performing on Minamo. It would have been almost worth it to watch Hidetsugu crunch Mochi up like a big blue icicle, but not quite.

"You have our thanks, ochimusha." Pearl-Ear bowed. "You have taken a great step forward in earning our trust."

"Not mine," Sharp-Ear called. "I still hate you."

"Should have left him behind," Toshi muttered. He returned Pearl-Ear's bow and said, "Thank you, Lady. I have changed much since I met you, and I think it's for the better."

Nearby, Sharp-Ear made a rude noise.

Pearl-Ear gracefully ignored her brother and spoke to Toshi. "What will you do now?"

"I still have some business to take care of."

Pearl-Ear lowered her voice. "Mochi?"

Toshi nodded. "I don't believe he was as helpless as he seemed. I may have surprised him at first, but it's just as likely he was waiting to see what I'd do so he could exploit it." He grinned. "I don't think he expected me to drop the daimyo's prize in his lap, in any case."

"Probably not. Wasn't it dangerous to just leave it with him like that?"

"Maybe, but I don't want it, and I didn't want Konda to have it. That thing's a trouble magnet."

"What do you think will become of it?"

"Oh, I'm sure someone will latch onto it. The world's full of fools. Eventually, O-Kagachi will catch up to it, slaughter who-ever has it, and that'll be that." He winked. "When and wherever that happens, I intend to be elsewhere."

Pearl-Ear watched him for a few moments. "A friendly word of advice, Toshi?"

"Mm?"

"You would do well to be less guarded and less flip. You have a way of speaking that always makes it seem as if you're up to something."

The ochimusha nodded soberly. "I'll work on that, Lady. Thank you."

* * * * *

Several hours later, Toshi was sitting in a cave beside a crackling fire. The cave was his, scouted years ago and stocked with enough provisions to last a month. More recently, he'd brought Michiko here after rescuing her from the snakefolk. It was here that he first encountered Mochi. It was here where he first accepted the Myojin of Night's Reach.

Toshi was naked to the waist as he stirred a stew pot above the fire. The kanji marks on his wrists, arms and forehead were all visible, but they itched uncomfortably. Toshi was still new to spiritual worship, but he recognized a clear sign when he saw it. Something was coming; someone was not quite finished with him yet.

Sure enough, the pressure dropped and a thin line of black thread crawled across the center of the cave at eye level. The thread doubled back on itself and returned to its starting point. It continued to travel back and forth, its speed increasing, until it had woven a solid black curtain across the rear of the enclosure.

Emaciated arms unfolded over the curtain and dozens of floating hands shimmered into view. A clean white speck formed at the center of the curtain, expanding to become a bone-white mask of a delicate female face.

The Myojin of Night's Reach floated before Toshi, patient as a stone.

"Hello," he said. He continued to stir his stew.

It is time, my acolyte. Are you prepared?

"I am. But first . . . you are adamant that this is necessary?"

I am. Your loyalty is a fickle, malleable thing. I would have you simplify your entanglements and clarify your dedication to me.

"I am your humble servant."

Servant, perhaps, but never humble. You may begin whenever you are ready.

Toshi left the spoon in the stew pot. Still not looking at the myojin, he rubbed his left wrist. He gazed into the fire, past it, and far beyond. Then he moved the stew pot to the cave floor and slid forward onto his knees.

His hand moved up to the kanji cut into his forearm. He closed his eyes and faded from sight. Still in the same position, Toshi extended his left hand into the fire. He rotated his wrist so that the back of his hand was directly over the flames. Slowly, bit by bit, Toshi willed himself solid.

He had been rubbing the hyozan tattoo on his hand with special oils and extracts for hours, chanting softly as he worked. He was real enough to be burned by the fire, but it caressed his hand rather than consuming it, the flame flowing around his skin without ever touching.

Toshi stopped reforming himself and started to fade once more. He could still see his hand in the fire, but the flames flickered through it without resistance. Toshi waited until a single tall flame danced steadily through the center of his palm. He began chanting again and with agonizing precision, slowly drew his hand out of the fire.

The hyozan tattoo seemed to snag on the tall spike of flame. Toshi eased his progress but kept pulling his hand away. The tattoo pulled free of his flesh, clinging like a scab as it detached from his hand.

Clean, unmarked, and unburned, Toshi pulled his hand away. In the crackling fire, the hyozan tattoo fluttered like a flag on a pole. The symbol caught fire, withered, and disappeared up through a hole in the roof with the rest of the smoke.

Well done, my acolyte. Now our real work can begin in earnest.

Toshi looked up at the wide curtain of black behind the white mask. In it, he saw visions, glimpses of things that were true or could soon be true.

He saw Konda leading an army of twisted ghosts to the edge of the Kamitaki Falls.

He saw soratami warriors in chariots, raining magic and destruction down on the Jukai Forest.

He saw a vast field of dead soldiers and bandits, each frozen solid with a look of mortal dread on their faces.

He saw the All-Consuming Oni of Chaos and O-Kagachi clashing in the sky under a crescent moon.

He saw himself, trapped between Kiku with her camellia on one side and Hidetsugu with his spiked tetsubo on the other.

And he saw Michiko, her eyes bright and terrible, as she raised her father's prize high overhead with both hands, preparing to dash it to the ground. There was blood on her hands and tears in her eyes.

"Yes," Toshi said out loud. He was free of the reckoners for the first time since his teens. He had earned the personal enmity of the daimyo and re-earned the personal trust of the princess. A primordial beast had come to destroy the world, provided an ancient oni didn't devour it first. And he was an open and declared enemy of both the soratami and their patron spirit.

He turned to the white mask, once more rubbing the back of his left hand.

"Yes," he said again. "Now our real work can begin."

As the Myojin of Night's Reach withdrew back into herself, Toshi wondered exactly what work she had in mind. He wondered how vastly her plans differed from his.

FROM *NEW YORK TIMES*

BEST-SELLING AUTHOR

R.A. SALVATORE

In taverns, around campfires, and in the loftiest council chambers of Faerûn, people whisper the tales of a lone dark elf who stumbled out of the merciless Underdark to the no less unforgiving wilderness of the World Above and carved a life for himself, then lived a legend...

THE LEGEND OF DRIZZT

For the first time in deluxe hardcover editions, all three volumes of the Dark Elf Trilogy take their rightful place at the beginning of one of the greatest fantasy epics of all time. Each title contains striking new cover art and portions of an all-new author interview, with the questions posed by none other than the readers themselves.

HOMELAND

Being born in Menzoberranzan means a hard life surrounded by evil.

EXILE

But the only thing worse is being driven from the city with hunters on your trail.

SOJOURN

Unless you can find your way out, never to return.

Legends Trilogy

Margaret Weis & Tracy Hickman

Each volume available for the first time ever in hardcover!

TIME OF THE TWINS
Volume I

Caramon Majere vows to protect Crysania, a
devout cleric, in her quest to save Raistlin from
himself. But both are soon caught in the dark
mage's deadly designs, and their one hope is a
frivolous kender.

WAR OF THE TWINS
Volume II

Catapulted through time by Raistlin's dark
magics, Caramon and Crysania are forced to aid
the mage in his quest to defeat the
Queen of Darkness.

TEST OF THE TWINS
Volume III

As Raistlin's plans come to fruition, Caramon
comes face to face with his destiny. Old friends
and strange allies come to aid him, but Caramon
must take the final step alone.